Praise for *Personal Velocity:*

"Rebecca Miller's debut story collection is a series of eye-opening portraits of women . . . humane, always honest and always entertaining."   —Mark Rozzo, *Los Angeles Times*

"*Personal Velocity* is a gutsy, striking debut."
                    —David Daley, *The Hartford Courant*

"Each story is crafted with a cunning and precision that explores and often explodes the lives of Miller's subjects, revealing their unusual motivations, perverse sorrows and simultaneous perceptions of both victory and loss."
                    —Laura Anderson, *American-Statesman*

"Miller tackles her topics, and ours, with wisdom sophistication and guts."   —*Glamour*

"While [Miller] has the ability to pare down her prose to the essentials, what makes her such a fine writer is how truly essential the resulting work is."
                    —Rob Thomas, *The Capital Times*

"Spare, elegant stories."   —*Kirkus Reviews*

"Each story is as sharply rendered and as neatly contained as a film shot. It is a shame to have to use the cliché *compulsively readable* to describe such an original collection."
                    —*Library Journal* (starred review)

"If I were still teaching high school English, I'd order class sets of Rebecca Miller's *Personal Velocity*. I'd want my students to follow Ms. Miller's journey into the human heart. I'd want them to see the power of simplicity in her writing. My students would surely realize that *Personal Velocity* is about them and their families, that this remarkable writer reveals what is under our noses. And isn't that the gift of the true artist?"

—Frank McCourt, author of *Angela's Ashes*

"Rebecca Miller's voice is distinctive in all cases, and her dialogue rings true across the board, whether she's writing about New York intellectuals or battered wives in the Midwest. These stories are richly evocative, sexy as hell, and thick with dramatic event. This is a startling debut."

—A. R. Gurney, author of *Love Letters*

"Rebecca Miller is a fearless, talented writer. In *Personal Velocity*, that fearlessness has led her to explore women's lives of great diversity and complexity, while her talent has made those lives indelible. A terrific debut."

—John Burnham Schwartz, author of *Bicycle Days* and *Claire Marvel: A Novel*

Personal Velocity

Personal
Velocity

Rebecca Miller

Grove Press   New York

Published simultaneously in Canada
Printed in the United States of America

Lyrics for "Baby's Got Her Blue Jeans On," words and music by Bob
McDill, copyright © 1984, are used courtesy of Universal-Polygram
International Publishing, Inc., o/b/o Itself and Ranger Bob Music
(ASCAP), International copyright secured. All Rights Reserved.

FIRST GROVE PRESS PAPERBACK EDITION

Library of Congress Cataloging-in-Publication Data

Miller, Rebecca.
     Personal velocity / Rebecca Miller.
        p. cm.
     ISBN 0-8021-3918-3 (pbk.)
     1. Women—Fiction.   I. Title.
   PS3613.I55 P47 2001
   813'.6—dc21   2001035093

Design by Laura Hammond Hough

Grove Press
841 Broadway
New York, NY 10003

02 03 04 05 06   10 9 8 7 6 5 4 3 2 1

For D.

Contents

Personal Velocity

Greta

Greta Herskovitz looked down at her husband's shoes one morning and saw with shocking clarity that she was going to leave him. The shoes were earnest, inexpensive brown wing tips. Greta was wearing a pair of pointy alligator flats. Lee was twenty-eight, the same age as Greta. He was six feet tall, had blond hair, powerful shoulders and a slender waist. His cheeks were peppered with pockmarks, but they looked good on him. Since he'd left graduate school, Lee had worked as a fact checker for *The New Yorker* and was whittling away at an eleven-hundred-page dissertation about two firsthand accounts of nineteenth-century Arctic expeditions and how they reflected Victorian society. The cannibalism in particular. Lee was a kind, quiet man. If he ever fell out of love with Greta, she knew he would go into therapy and fix it. But she hadn't bargained on her own success.

One day about a year prior to the moment with the shoes, Greta was walking down the hall of the shabby, venerable publishing firm Warren and Howe in a pair of cheap pumps, carrying an untidy pile of seven file folders, each containing a different recipe for rice pudding. She was currently editing a book by Tammy Lee Felber entitled *Three Hundred and Sixty-Five Ways to Cook Rice*. Aaron Gelb, the legendary senior editor at Warren and Howe, a wise, sad man with enormous pockets under his brown eyes and a slow, pessimistic, humorous pattern of speech, called out to her from his office.

"Ms. Herskovitz," he said, "would you come in here please?"

Greta turned, alarmed. She was wearing a fitted brown suit with a skirt that ended several inches above the knees, and she wondered if maybe she was pushing it. As she entered, Mr. Gelb sat down at his desk and put his head in his hands, his customary posture when in thought. Greta sat down opposite him. Her nylons rubbed together as she crossed her legs. Worried that her skirt looked obscene, she gave it a little tug. Mr. Gelb slipped his glasses to the top of his head, rubbing his eyes for a very long time and sighing. Then he looked out the window.

"Thavi Matola wants to have lunch with you," he said.

Thavi Matola was the hottest writer of his generation. He was thirty-three. Greta's publishing house wanted him badly. They were calling his agent, trying to get to him through his friends. His first novel, *Blue Mountain,* was a love story about

Bounmy, a Laotian male prostitute, and an Alabama gas-station attendant named Rory. It had won the PEN Faulkner Prize, sold half a million copies.

"With me?" Greta said.

"He called me up and said he heard we had an excellent editor here. And it was you." Greta had never edited anything but cookbooks. "Do you have any idea why he might have said that?"

"Maybe he likes to cook," said Greta. Mr. Gelb smiled faintly.

"If the lunch goes well, he'll come to Warren and Howe. If not, he'll go peddle his wounded psyche someplace else."

"Wow," said Greta. "This is really strange."

"One o'clock on Thursday at the Senate," Gelb said, opening a drawer and taking out a large roll of antacid tablets. "Wear pants." Greta got up. When she was at the door, Gelb said, "Wear what you want. What do I know." She shut the door. Poor Mr. Gelb. She went straight out to the most expensive shoe store she had ever heard of and put the alligator flats on her credit card. She couldn't even begin to afford them, but she needed to feel worthy, she needed to feel like a pro.

On the day of the meeting she wore a red suit with a fairly short skirt—just above the knees. It was a cool, clear spring day. She was twenty minutes early, so she walked over to the

Museum of Modern Art and wandered around the cluttered
gift shop with the fixed stare of a sleepwalker, little charges
of anxiety going off in her belly, till three minutes to one.
Then she rushed over to the restaurant, sat down at the corner table that had been reserved by Mr. Gelb's secretary, and
took out her notebook so she'd look busy. Inside was a shopping list: bananas, clementines, toilet paper, rice, batteries,
tampons. She looked up and Thavi Matola was standing there.

"Greta Herskovitz?" he said.

"Yes—oh, hi!" Greta stood up, adjusting her hair band. She
felt off-kilter. She should have been watching for him. Thavi
sat down. He was slender, androgynous-looking, with smooth
brown skin and short curly hair. His mother was Laotian, Greta
remembered. Father, Italian-American soldier, dead. Refu-
gees. Hard life. Three sisters, two left behind in Laos because
of that government.

"I really loved your first book," she said.

"It's a piece of shit," said Thavi in a slight accent, lighting a cigarette.

"I think that's pretty common," said Greta.

"Second thoughts?"

"Self-hatred." A minor convulsion of amusement forced
the smoke out of Matola's nose; he fixed his gaze on Greta
like a child surprised to hear a stranger call him by his nick-
name. Greta felt her muscles relax. "The pasta's good here,"

she said, then ordered steak frites. Thavi convulsed again, air hissing from his nostrils, lips clamped shut. They started a bottle of wine. Greta didn't usually drink at lunch but she could tell he wanted to so she went with it, trying hard not to let her mind go slack.

"What's the new book about?" she asked. "If you don't mind talking about it."

"Laos," he said. "The trip over. I was on my own."

"That must have been frightening," said Greta. "How old were you?"

"Thirteen," he said.

"Have you written much yet?"

"About a hundred pages. Aren't I the one supposed to be asking the questions?"

"I don't know," she said.

"What's your story?" he asked.

"Manhattan, I was born in Manhattan, went to the Flemming School uptown—a small private, you know—and then to boarding school, then to college, then to law school, but I quit—my father's a lawyer, we're not speaking, my mother is—well, dead. They're divorced. I mean they were. I'm twenty-eight. My father has a three-year-old." *God almighty please let me shut up,* she thought. Her steak arrived. She cut into it vigorously.

"My friend Felicia Wong said you were great at trimming

fat," he said, watching her do so. Felicia Wong had written short stories at Harvard. Greta had been one of the editors of *The Advocate*. She had an eye for the inessential and would sift through the undergraduate fiction, culling every superfluous word. The writers had called her the Grim Reaper. Yet they all wanted Greta Herskovitz to comb through their work. She had been a bit of a star at Harvard.

"I have a tendency to overwrite," he said. "I need someone to kick my ass."

"I can kick your ass," said Greta accommodatingly, wondering if he was gay. By the time she got back to the office, Thavi Matola had called and said he'd sign with Warren and Howe if Greta Herskovitz edited the book. It was unbelievable. No more rice pudding. All the other editors came into her cubicle to congratulate her. Miss Pells, the sixty-five-year-old receptionist, showed Greta where her new office was going to be. She'd have a door, a window. Before Greta left, Gelb called her into his office.

"We'll renegotiate your contract next week," he said, looking impressed and suspicious. It was surreal.

When she got home Lee was watching a documentary about boat building. Greta burst into the room, dropping her bag on the floor, yelling, "HE WANTS ME TO DO IT!"

"That's amazing, sweetheart," he said. Greta saw a shadow of anxiety cross Lee's face, and she blushed, feeling strangely sheepish. As they talked over her triumph quietly on the couch, a toxic blend of anxiety and elation built up in Greta's mind and seemed actually to be pressing against her skull. She craved air. She wanted to go out, she wanted to tell people her news, she wanted to get drunk, to celebrate. She remembered a party uptown being given by an old friend from Exeter, a girl named Mimi. Mimi was tall and thin, very blond, and so beautiful it was hard to look at her. She was, however, uneasy in herself, and had a tendency to join cults, which was to Greta a small consolation. Greta was squat, with short muscular legs and thick dark hair and squinty brown eyes and full lips. And charisma. Many men found her sexy. Her boyfriends had tended to leave her, though, for girls like Mimi. The fragile kind.

At the party, Lee was having a laconic conversation with a couple of playwrights they both knew. Greta watched him as he talked. Lee's words were so carefully chosen that sometimes she imagined his ideas having to stand in line for inspection before they could be expressed. The delay must have been agonizing. As a rule Greta found Lee's withholding of language sexy. But tonight she was restless. She squeezed his hand and wandered off to explore the apartment, buoyed by her news. Mimi's bedroom door was open so Greta walked in to look at the photographs she'd glimpsed from the hall. She had always been curious about Mimi. As she peered into a silver-framed portrait of a portly Indian man in a robe, she heard a rustling behind her. She turned and saw Oscar Levy. Oscar had been a suitor of Greta's at Harvard, but she'd never slept with him. He was funny and pessimistic, a first violinist with some important orchestra now, Greta couldn't remember which one. He stood behind her in his rumpled gray tweed jacket and black turtleneck, holding a beer.

"Oscar!" Greta said. "God, you scared me."

"You scared me, too," he said.

They chatted for a while, sitting on Mimi's chaotic bed. The room stank of incense. There was a gentle neutrality in Oscar's tone that Greta didn't recognize. He was speaking to her as one speaks to someone who has been mentally ill or had cancer. She knew why, too. It was because she had turned out to be a loser. Greta thought of Lee in the other room, conversing tersely, groping behind him for her hand expectantly like a child on a shopping trip.

"I was sorry to hear about your mother," Oscar said.

"Thanks," said Greta flatly, looking at the little mole above his lip.

"Your husband seems like a really nice guy," he said. "I've just been talking to him."

"He'll never leave me," she said, and blushed, shocked by her own candor.

"That seems like a weird reason to—"

"It's not the main reason. I love him. I think he's funny. We have a good time. He's a wonderful person."

"Okay, okay," he said.

"What about you," she asked, "are you—"

"God no—I'm only twenty-eight!"

"So am I, Oscar. Do you have a girlfriend?"

"Yes. We don't see each other much. She's with the Boston Symphony. I'm with the Brooklyn."

"Oh." His sneaky boast irritated her.

"Are you still with that publishing company . . ."

"Warren and Howe. Actually I just found out I'm going to be editing Thavi Matola's new book," she said. There was a pause.

"The guy who wrote *Blue Mountain*?"

"Yeah."

"Wow. That's amazing." He looked at her as if her seductiveness was being refueled before his eyes. She suddenly felt angry at herself and got up. "I should get back," she said. She went to Lee, holding his hand, her head on his shoulder. At ten o'clock Lee went home because he had to get up early and call an author in Nova Scotia to check facts about a fly-fishing article. Greta hung around for another hour, speaking to people absentmindedly as she watched Mimi giggling in her floor-length orange robe, a photograph of an old man hanging in a pendant around her neck. As she walked out the door Oscar was behind her. "You want to share a cab?" he asked. On the ride downtown, as they drove by the park, Oscar leaned over and kissed her. Greta parted her lips; his tongue reached out tentatively, like a snail, and started poking around blindly inside her mouth. He tasted faintly of metal. The cab stopped at his apartment building.

"Come in," he whispered.

"I can't," she said. She wanted to go home. She wanted to pretend this hadn't happened.

"Come on. One conversation."

"No. Sorry. Please." She pulled the cab door shut.

"Ninth Street and First Avenue," she said. The cab sped off. Greta leaned back and shut her eyes, sinking into a pit of self-recrimination. *Shit, shit, shit, shit,* she thought. She hadn't slipped up once since the wedding. But it had been a problem before.

Three years earlier, seven days before she married Lee, Greta was sitting in a pastry shop near Columbia reading when a young man in a vintage tweed coat walked up to her table and asked her if she had a cigarette. He was in his late twenties, slender, clearly Jewish, and he looked like he had a cold. Behind him through the plateglass window Greta could see fine snow swirling through the dusk.

"I don't smoke," she said.

"Too bad," said the young man.

"I actually think I should be congratulated," said Greta.

"Why, did you quit?"

"I was never really addicted. I used to smoke occasionally, then it struck me that it was idiotic." *Oops*, she thought. Greta was always insulting people without meaning to, especially men. Even when she was eleven, slights were her way of flirting. Which explained why she had so few dates until she went to college. "I mean," she said, "it wouldn't have been idiotic if I had actually been addicted. Then it would have been pathetic." The young man was staring at her now, a bemused smile on his face. "I'm sorry," Greta said, blushing. "I just got out of a shrink appointment." She wished she was on the subway, a sure sign that she was having a bad time.

"You don't have to apologize," he said, laughing. "It's a stupid habit and I'm stopping when I turn thirty."

"When do you turn thirty?"

"Seven days."

"The twenty-third?"

"Yes," he said.

"I'm getting married on the twenty-third."

"Oh!" he said, averting his gaze. "Terrific! Maybe we should celebrate together."

"Yes. An abstinence party."

"Well, good luck."

"Thanks." He walked over to the counter where the pastries were displayed and asked for a cup of coffee. Greta opened her novel. Out of the corner of her eye she watched the young man take his cup, sit down, and remove some papers and a fountain pen from a battered leather shoulder bag. He became immersed in his work immediately and seemed to have forgotten all about her. *Married/invisible,* Greta thought as she drained her cup and put on her heavy camel-hair coat. As she passed him she said, "Bye."

"Bye," he said with a pleasant smile, a smile reserved for married women and aunts. It was nearly dark now. Greta walked down the block, her mind congealed around the image of the young man seated at his table ignoring her. She walked as one hypnotized into the bodega on the corner and asked for a pack of Camel Lights. Three dollars and seventy-five cents! She had stopped smoking when they were one-seventy-five. She took the cigarettes and shoved them into the pocket of her coat, shouldering the wind as she trudged back up the block to the pastry shop, opened the door, walked over to the young man, who was writing into a leather-bound notebook, and set the packet of cigarettes gently down in front of him like a bird dog releasing a partridge from its mouth. The young man looked up at her quizzically, then smiled.

They smoked together and talked for an hour. His name was Max. He was a theological student at Columbia, wanted to be a rabbi. Greta let out a shriek when he told her.

"You don't look like a rabbi," she said.

"I'm not Orthodox," he said, grinning, his hand on her thigh. Greta called Lee from a pay phone and said she was spending the night with her maid of honor. The rest of the week was a tangle of wedding preparations and subterfuge. It never occurred to Greta to call off the marriage because she was having an affair. She kept the two narratives distinct in her mind; they coexisted as if in twin universes separated by a vast field of space. The only trouble was that Greta was exhausted, what with traveling uptown to Max and downtown to Lee, the fittings, the fucking, the dinners, the bachelorette party, and the cold that Max had given her. Only her trusted, worldly friend Lola Sanduli, who understood Greta better than anyone, knew about Max, and Lola felt that the whole thing was harmless. It was just Greta being Greta. And indeed, at the end of that crazy week, as Greta sat smoking one last cigarette with her lover at the Hungarian pastry shop, an hour before she had to take a cab to the airport so she could marry Lee in Ohio, Greta was going over and over the things she'd packed for the wedding, wondering if she'd forgotten anything. She was excited to be getting married and felt very much in love. With Lee. The week with Max had left her feeling absolutely gorgeous. Now she wished he would disappear. But Max was very much extant, staring glumly at his coffee cup, his thin, pale face and black curls making him look like a Spanish Christ, of all things. At last he spoke, breaking her concentration.

"Is he even Jewish?"

"No. What difference does that make?" Greta asked, irritated.

"It makes a difference."

"You really are a rabbi," she said, smiling.

"Well," Max said sadly, "I hope you're happy."

Why the hell had she kissed Oscar Levy? Yuck. The cab pounded its way down Broadway, its suspension shot. Greta's cheeks burned with remorse. The truth is that for some time now she had been dimly aware of a darkness gnawing at the edge of her mind, a gathering blackness that she couldn't name, but she felt it as a hole, an emptiness into which something alien might step. It was a kind of hunger.

. . .

Lee was asleep when she came home. When she woke up, he was on the phone in the living room.

"A 'Connamaragh Black,'" he was saying, "is for . . . right. Exclusively? . . . Okay. Okay, yes. . . ." Greta went to Lee and curled up on the floor, her arms around his strong calves. He leaned down and stroked her head. "I see," he said. "Right. I think that's it, Mr. Conway, thank you for your time. Good luck with the fish this morning. Bye." He hung up the phone.

"What's the matter?" he said.

"I feel yucky," she said.

"You want me to make you pancakes?" Greta nodded, crawling into his lap and burying her head in his chest.

"I love you so much," she said.

Greta had decided to marry Lee on a trip to Ohio to visit his parents. His family lived on the border of Kentucky, and his strawberry-blond high school girlfriend Kelly had a charming southern accent and perfect limbs.

"Why do you love *me*?" Greta had asked Lee as they poured over pictures of him tossing footballs, accepting awards, holding his blue-eyed girlfriend's hand on prom night. "I'm just a nasty little black-eyed dwarf." He kissed her forehead.

"I love my nasty dwarf," he said. And he did love her. But Greta was suspicious. She became jealous of everything and everyone out of Lee's past. Lee took on a power in her eyes, the power of having been loved by a girl with blond eyelashes, of having grown up among these mystical beasts, slow-moving, broad-browed Germanic people who said grace and "please pass the bread, Mom," who weren't always yelling out

ideas over dinner like they were selling fish in a souk. After
four solid days of Ohio Greta felt so intensely in love that she
wanted to elope. But they ended up having a proper white
wedding in a country church in Ironton, a hundred yards from
the golf course where Lee had lost his virginity to the girl with
blond eyelashes. Greta was wearing a vast white dress. After
they'd said their vows she turned around and saw her father.
He looked annoyed. Tears stung her eyes.

Avram Herskovitz didn't think much of Lee Schneeweiss.
He didn't think Lee had size. Everybody in the Herskovitz clan
had to have size. Avram had white, sharp teeth, a booming
voice, burning black eyes. He never put on weight. He was
one of the best-known lawyers in the country, a self-made
man. He defended the indefensible. He was on the news a
lot, standing on some court steps, saying, "This decision is
a victory for justice in this country." Many people thought
he was a moral giant. Others thought he was a cynic who
didn't care about guilt or innocence, only about winning.
Greta knew he was both of these things. Avram Herskovitz
had been forty when he married Greta's mother, Maroushka.
Maroushka had been twenty-five, a tender-eyed Polish girl,
born in Auschwitz two days before the arrival of the Russians.
Her father, a professor of ethnology, had been gassed a week
before her birth. After the liberation, Maroushka's mother

went quietly insane, and Maroushka was brought up in a series of orphanages. This story stirred some deep yearning in Avram. He had to save this woman, he had to give her a beautiful life. He brushed off his first family like leaves from a sweater. When Greta was born he cherished her. She was his new beginning, life sprung from the ash heap. He held her up above the waves on the beach. They were inseparable, alike. As unconsciously as a leaf unfurling, young Greta chose to embody her father's charming voraciousness, shrinking instinctively from the wistful sweetness of her mother, smelling as it did, ever so faintly, of death. Then when Greta was twenty-one, a dogged and rapacious law student, she came back to Nantucket for the summer, as she had every year since she was three, with some tremendous news: a paper she'd written on capital punishment was going to be published in the *Harvard Law Review*. She entered the hall, smelling the familiar mixture of must and potpourri, threw her bags down and charged into the living room, triumphant. Her father was standing by the window, watching the calm sea. A slight breeze fluttered the yellow curtains. Avram turned and looked at his precious daughter with a strange, pained expression. Greta could feel that she had interrupted something. On the couch at the other end of the room, her elbows on her knees, head in her hands, was a young woman. She looked up at Greta. The young woman had green eyes, a thin face, curly dark hair, and a slender, wiry body. She was wearing white linen pants and a striped cotton T-shirt. Greta felt a terrible aching deep in her gut.

"Where's Mom?" she said.

"I think she's in the kitchen," her father said softly. Turning, almost unable to move, Greta walked stiffly into the kitchen. Maroushka stood in the center of the room, arms limp at her sides, her slender body as erect and graceful as a Degas dancer, an expression of shocked acceptance on her face. It was as if the death sentence that she had been waiting for all her life had finally been handed down. Greta went to her mother and hugged her. Maroushka's form felt so insubstantial, so light. It felt as though she could come apart in Greta's hands.

Greta had trouble concentrating after the divorce. She wandered around campus, spent whole hours staring in cafés. She'd stopped speaking to Avram, returned his monthly checks unopened. Then one day she dropped out of law school. She couldn't lend meaning to the words anymore. That November Maroushka was diagnosed with cancer. Greta moved back to New York to be with her, took a series of jobs in magazines, had a couple of boyfriends, lost them. Maroushka died. Avram's wife had a baby girl. Then Greta met Lee through a friend from Harvard. From their first conversation Greta wanted to be with him all the time. Just listening to his middle American voice

made her feel safe. His lack of ambition struck her as spiritu-
ally advanced. Avram took Greta's new life as a personal
affront. His brilliant daughter was wasting herself out of
spite. The bland midwestern boyfriend seemed proof of her
vendetta against him.

. . .

The night before she was married Greta had the following dream: She was in the house in Nantucket with her father and Lee. As they watched the evening news her father
said casually, "I think I'll kill myself after dinner."

"Good idea," said Lee, looking over at Greta amiably. "I'll
kill Greta." Greta tried to smile in the dream but she was
terrified. She escaped from the house and ran toward a di-
lapidated barn at the top of a small hill. It was dusk by now.
She charged into the barn, panting. Immediately she understood that it was a kibbutz. There was a fat, slovenly man
standing at a high desk.

"Please!" said Greta. "Help me! My fiancé is going to kill
me. I have to call the police. Can I use the phone?" Irritated,
the man picked up the phone and dialed 911.

"Call me back," he said, and hung up. Greta assumed that
911 calls must be very expensive. Just then an enormous
group of people bustled past Greta and she got pushed into
a large van. Before she knew it she was on vacation with the

kibbutz. A woman was driving. She was enormous, her dark sweaty hair swept back in a careless ponytail, her massive shoulders sloped forward as she leaned into the steering wheel. Greta was seated between a courting couple who insisted on kissing behind her back. The van stopped at a broken-down motel and everyone—there were about fifteen kids—clawed their way out. In the motel restaurant Greta sat miserably on the sticky Naugahyde seat, nursing a club soda. No one was paying any attention to her, or even wondering what she was doing there. They were all devouring some meaty substance, picking up the chunks with their hands. Now Mr. Gelb walked over and sat down at the booth.

"I hear you're having a bad time," he said.

"It's not that," said Greta. "We get along really well. It's just that he said he was going to kill me." Lee walked in now, smiling. Greta was awash with relief and threw herself on his neck. They were as close as ever. It *had* been a joke. Just as they were leaving the restaurant, arm in arm, the father of the family stood up, his massive belly coming almost to his knees.

"Wait a minute," he said. "You owe me two hundred dollars!"

"What?" said Greta.

"For dinner, gas . . ."

"But I didn't eat anything!"

"All right. Twenty bucks for gas then. And the club soda."

Greta woke up laughing, Lee beside her.

"I just had the most anti-Semitic dream, it was so—oh my God, it's so bad!"

. . .

Strangely, Greta had never felt particularly Jewish. Her parents hadn't ever brought her to a synagogue—being Jewish was taken for granted in the family, like having skin. A Catholic schoolmate, Kate Donovan, had lived on the floor below the Herskovitzes on Park Avenue, and Greta often accompanied her to church. During the service she would always pretend she was a member of Kate's large, freckled family. Her fantasy was ruptured each week, however, when each of the ruddy Donovans rose to take communion, filing by her one by one, until only Greta was left kneeling, watching the long line of lucky club members waiting for their wafers and wine. She would duck her head and move her lips at these moments, pretending that she hadn't gone to confession that week and so was not eligible to take the host. When Greta thought about being Jewish she thought of a dark room with an old lady in a rocking chair in the corner. She didn't know why. Once, as she ate raw cookie dough with Kate in the Donovans' orange kitchen, she heard Mr. Donovan say, "Something something damn Jews," in the next room, and

his wife had said, "Norman!" very gently. Greta blushed scar-
let, feeling a visceral sense of shame. It was the only moment
in her life when she felt absolutely Jewish, right down to the
tips of her toes.

The first two years of marriage with Lee were blissful.
They fixed up their East Village apartment with little white
Christmas lights and covered the tattered couches in heavy
white cloth. They resanded the floors and hung paintings
by their friends on the walls. Greta got a job as a copy editor at Warren and Howe and eventually Mr. Gelb asked her
if she knew anything about cooking. She did—Maroushka
had taught her. She got promoted. She didn't really care,
though she liked the extra cash. With relief Greta felt the
ambition draining out of her like pus from a lanced boil. She
had stopped desiring other men. She wanted to have a baby.
She was going to lead a simple, decent life. The marriage
had worked like a magical charm.

. . .

Thavi Matola's writing about his escape from Laos was
exquisite and filled with pain but there were patches of fat
and confusion. Thavi encouraged Greta to make radical suggestions for rewrites. They met a couple of times a week. The
red walls of his apartment made Greta feel like a surgeon who
has entered the body of her patient; his sentences bound her

like veins. She cut the veins and they bled words. At night when she looked up at Lee after reading the manuscript for hours, she had trouble focusing her eyes on him. Lee's voice actually seemed to have gotten fainter; she found herself asking him to repeat himself all the time, to the point where they both worried for her hearing.

One night as they ate together in silence, Lee asked, "How long is it going to take Matola to finish this book?"

"I have no idea," she said.

"It could take years, right?"

"Not everyone writes as slowly as you do," she said, grabbing for his hand immediately and smiling. But it was too late. She'd hurt him. Greta lay awake for hours that night, Lee asleep beside her, his long lithe arms thrown out above his blond head, his face young and smooth. Even in sleep he looked blameless as a baby. Sweating now, a taste like manure in her mouth, Greta felt like a sticky little gremlin crouching beside Apollo. She walked into the living room to make a cup of tea. Lee's dissertation was lying open at his desk in the corner of the room. Greta walked over to it and switched on the light, perversely drawn to the text. She'd read bits of it over the years but a tacit agreement had grown up between them that she wouldn't look at it until he was finished. As she read now it was all she could do to stop herself from crossing out whole paragraphs. The thing was swollen to bursting with redundancies. She found his language both naive and pompous with its old-fashioned academic flourishes. Greta wondered if it wasn't fear that prevented Lee from cutting his dissertation down to a presentable length and ending his days as a permanent student. Once he had his Ph.D., he'd have to start applying for teaching jobs. He'd have to rustle up a little drive. *If he would just let me have it for a week,* she thought to herself, *he'd have his Ph.D. by Christmas.* But he wouldn't let her have it, nor should he. She knew very little about the subject. She just knew language. It was a curse in a way. *Why can't he write like he talks,* she thought. The kettle boiled. She walked away.

A few days later Thavi was sitting on the floor of his apartment, reading Greta's notes when he asked, "How does your husband feel about us working together like this?"

"Fine, I think," said Greta, looking down at him from the couch.

"Why isn't he jealous?" he asked with mock pique.

"I told him you were gay," she said teasingly.

"Is that what you think?"

"I vacillate," said Greta.

"So do I," said Thavi. Her bare foot was next to him on the rug. He stroked the top of it very gingerly. She slid off the couch and sat next to him on the floor. They kissed, grop-

ing furiously. Greta kept her hands above Thavi's waist. For
some reason she was embarrassed to touch him below it. After
a while they stopped and looked at each other, panting.

"You want some juice?" he asked. He poured her some
and they went back to work. As the weeks wore on the groping continued. They didn't talk about it; every now and then
they would fall into each other's arms and make out, then
stop, like a stalled car. At home in bed with Lee Greta felt
spikes of violence rising in her suddenly like nausea while they
were making love. She would push Lee, scratch him. She
wanted him to pin her down and bite her, to rend the cocoon
that she was weaving around herself. But he would never push
back, he would never pin her down. He would hold her gently and whisper, "What's the matter, baby?" A scream of frus-
tration pressed against her throat at these moments; she
clamped down her teeth, strangling it.

One night Greta got home at ten-thirty from working
with Thavi. Lee was sitting in the living room with his friend
Darius. Darius read scripts for Miramax and always had good
gossip about the movie business. He had gray teeth. Greta
had always found him pathetic. She greeted them both, went
into the bathroom, grabbed a towel from the rack, and threw
it down on the floor in front of the bathtub. Then she lay down
on the towel, pulled off her tights and her underwear, and

masturbated. She couldn't let herself think of Thavi so she thought about a stranger, a man with no face fucking her up against a wall. The orgasm was violent. When she came out she poured herself a glass of orange juice and sat down on the couch.

. . .

Thavi Matola's book was hailed as a masterpiece and sold big. Thavi thanked Greta warmly in the acknowledgments. A week after the book was reviewed Greta had an offer from another publishing house. They wanted her to come and work as one of their senior editors for an enormous pay hike. Greta gave Gelb a chance to match it. When he balked, she took the new job and Thavi left with her. When Greta's father heard the news, he insisted on throwing a party. His apartment was on Fifth Avenue and Ninety-sixth Street, a vast duplex with enormous eighteenth-century paintings on the walls. Avram's wiry wife greeted Greta and Lee with two glasses of champagne, three-year-old Anya clinging to her leg. Then Avram came out of his study, his arms outstretched, and embraced Greta, shutting his eyes tight. She hadn't let him get this close to her in years. She could feel the coarse black hair popping over his collar, scratching her cheek.

The first couple to arrive were Marvin and Dot Green, a couple Greta had known all her life. Marvin, a small, quiet, and very powerful man, was one of the great investment bankers of the last decade. Dot, a brash blond from Miami with great legs and mesmerizing stories about Florida high society in the 1950s, ran to Greta, greeting her as one thought lost in some terrible sea tragedy. Greta knew what Dot meant. Since she'd dropped out of law school Avram and Maroushka Herskovitz's daughter had been written off as one of those children not gifted or tough enough to survive so close to the brilliant light of their parents' world, one of those who had drifted down to live among the bottom feeders. But Greta's success had buoyed her back up from the depths. She had risen like some bubble belched out of the guts of a giant stingray, and here she was in the light again, with the sharks. As the guests arrived, it became clear that this was a party for Avram; they were all his old friends, some of the finest lawyers and politicians and businessmen in New York City, each of them rich. Greta had grown up with their children. It was touching in a way: Avram was showing his friends that his daughter was a success, that she had come back to him, and that she loved him. At one point during dinner someone made a crack about Greta playing dead all those years and now look at her.

"Well," Avram said, putting his arm around Greta's shoulders. "Everyone has their own personal velocity." It occurred to Greta that in this very room she could probably find enough investors to start her own publishing house one day. Her eye fell on Lee, who was stooped, listening to an elegant matron with a serious, considerate look on his face. Her heart ached for him. When it was time to go, she couldn't see Lee anywhere. She finally found him in the kitchen having a conversation with the barman. It turned out they'd gone to college together.

On the cab ride home, Greta reached over and held Lee's hand.

"It was sweet of my dad to throw me that party," she said. In her chest she felt the dull weight of alienation, as if someone were sitting on her sternum.

"Yeah," said Lee.

"Even if they were all his friends. Did you have an okay time?"

"It was fine," said Lee softly. "Now that you're done . . . maybe we could go away for a while."

"Mmm," she said, wondering how he could possibly still love her. If he did it was because he didn't know her. She was rotten with ambition, a lusty little troll, the kind of demon you'd find at the bottom floor of hell pulling fingernails off the loan sharks. When she got into bed Lee turned over slowly and pulled her toward him, kissing her. Suddenly he became very aroused. She tried hard to stay with it. Her mind was swarming with images—Dot Green's big teeth, her father hugging her, her father's wife grinning at her from across the room. Afterward, as she lay in the crook of Lee's arm, she felt safe and content, almost as she had when they first met. She clutched at the feeling as it faded; it was precious to her.

In the morning, she showered and dressed for the new job. When she came out of the bedroom Lee was already reading the paper. The coffee had been made and there was a brown paper bag full of fresh muffins on the table. Greta kissed Lee on the head, took a muffin, and poured milk into her coffee, observing the light that spilled sparkling through the window onto the blond wood table, the white china, Lee's white shirt, his golden hair. And then she looked down at his shoes. Suddenly a terrifying thought came into Greta's mind, clear and cruel. Tears of shame filled her eyes. She was going to dump her beautiful husband like a redundant paragraph. She reached out impulsively, as if she'd stumbled, and grabbed his arm.

"What is it?" he asked. But it was too late. Greta felt herself falling away at tremendous speed, her hair whipped back, the skin vibrating against her face. There was nothing she could do.

Delia

Delia Shunt was twenty-nine. She had fine, dirty-blond hair
and a strong, heavy ass that looked perfect in blue jeans. Her
breasts were soft and large for her small frame. She had a
slight overbite and green squinting eyes. She walked dead
straight, shoulders slightly stooped and squared like a man,
and smoked with her thumb and her forefinger. In five years
she would look forty but right now she looked hot and she
was aware of that fact. And Delia was mean. She beat up a
guy in a bar once just for grabbing her ass. Hit him right in
the face. He hit her back and she broke a chair over his head.

Delia had three children, two boys and a little girl, May.
May was rough like Delia and so was the older boy, John. But
Winslow, the middle one, was a dreamy child, and Delia
worried about his future. Her husband, Kurt, worked as a
switch operator on the railroad that snaked through town until
they caught him drinking and he moved on to work as a se-
curity guard for Safeway. Kurt used to beat Delia and she took
it for eight years until one night he grabbed her by the hair

and started banging her head against the kitchen table during dinner. They were having chicken. He knocked two teeth out of the side of her mouth and locked Delia in the basement. Then he started sobbing outside the door like a baby, scared to face what he'd done. Delia spent two hours collapsed against the basement door, telling Kurt in a firm, sane voice that everything was okay, she knew he didn't mean it, everything was going to go right back to normal if he would just unlock the door. The kids were howling, terrified. It was their pain that finally broke through Delia's inertia. Listening to her babies screaming and pleading and being unable to comfort them was like being murdered slowly; Delia held her head clamped between her hands and rocked herself back and forth. After two hours it didn't matter that she loved her husband, it didn't matter that she had no place to go. She was taking her kids away.

Eventually Kurt unlocked the door to the basement without saying a word and went into the den with a drink. Delia went into the bathroom, washed out her mouth, cleaned the blood off her face with cotton balls and antiseptic. Then she put the kids to bed and started folding laundry in the kitchen. Her hands were shaking. She could hear Kurt weeping in the next room. He was waiting for her to come in so she could forgive him like she usually did. She wanted to, but she didn't let herself. Eventually Kurt fell asleep. She poked him to make sure. Then she shoved some clothes in a suitcase and stood in the doorway of the children's room. May and John were sleeping in their beds, but Winslow was awake, staring out the window at the old oak tree that grew there. He loved to hear the leaves rustle.

"Honey," Delia whispered. "We have to go."

Winslow didn't say anything, he just got up off the bed and took his mother's hand. Delia felt tears sting her swollen eye but she wasn't about to start crying now.

"Okay, baby. We don't have much time."

She picked up little May, sticky with sleep. John rubbed his eyes.

"Is Daddy coming?" he whispered.

"No. Not yet."

"Are we running away?" John adored his father.

"We just have to go, John, now don't make me mad."

Delia sneaked the kids out of the house and into the car. Then she drove to Tucson, to the women's shelter there. She had driven by it many times. It was a concrete bunker with no windows, the saddest-looking building she had ever seen. There was no sign, no number on the door. That night she rang the bell and heard footsteps from inside. It was three o'clock in the morning. Three bolts slid back and a large woman with cropped hair wearing black sweatpants and a black T-shirt with the Starbucks logo on it opened the door and made a hurried gesture for them all to come in. The woman looked around behind them for a couple of seconds before closing the door and bolting it shut again.

"Do you think you were followed?" she asked.

"No" said Delia. "He was asleep." Her *s*'s were slurred and she remembered her missing teeth. Her eye was beginning to close. The woman looked at Delia's face without expression but there was pain in her eyes.

"We'll get you looked at in the morning." Delia's children were silent and stared wide-eyed into the body of the building. It smelled like a school.

The social worker at the shelter said she couldn't understand how such a strong woman could let herself get hit for so long. Delia thought for a minute.

"I guess I don't give up that easy," she said. Delia didn't like the social worker very much. Her name was Pam. She was thin, with a little shrew face and lank blond hair. She kept smiling, she smiled all the time, to the point where it was hard to understand what she was saying sometimes. Once Delia was smoking on the turquoise couch in the lounge when Pam came in with her clipboard and sat down in a molded-plastic chair opposite her. Delia didn't move, she just sat there looking at Pam. Pam sat smiling with her lips shut, beaming at Delia. Through the glass windows behind Pam Delia could see women shuffling up and down the corridor in their slippers like depressed nuns. May and John went running by, followed by three skinny kids wearing dirty clothes. Delia felt a little itch of irritation she'd felt so many times with Kurt— she was going to say something nasty.

"It must feel nice to be doing good twenty-four hours a day," Delia said.

"Oh, I don't know," said Pam. "Some days I don't think it makes any difference." The smile came and went in the space of an instant.

"Does that get you down, Pam?" said Delia.

"Sometimes—sometimes."

"You look like you never get down. You look like you're always happy."

"Everybody has problems, Delia." A pause. Delia wondered what Pam's problems could be. Dry cleaning probably wasn't ready for her big date.

"Have you ever been in love with a man who hit you?" Delia asked.

"No," Pam blushed.

"Do you have any kids?"

"No, I don't."

"Then leave me alone. I'm sick of seeing you every fucking day smiling like you just took the greatest shit of your life."

Red blotches appeared on Pam's cheeks and forehead.

God I'm a bitch, thought Delia.

Pam shifted in her chair and looked at the floor.

"Have you thought about another place to live when you leave?" There was a sharpness to her tone now. Delia almost smiled with relief. She hadn't creamed her after all.

"I guess I could stay with my dad . . ." She couldn't, but it was something to say.

"Don't you think your husband might come and make it—would he be a problem?" Delia let out a snort. Every day since she'd been at the shelter Kurt had been ringing the bell trying to sweet-talk the staff into letting him at least see his kids. Delia knew he would take them if he saw them and cave her head in if he saw her. The past was gone, irretrievable—severed with one turn of the ignition key. The problem now was where to go. She had been racking her brain for someone who could take them in, someone far away. Delia didn't have many allies. She'd had one visit in two weeks at the shelter—her mother, Marjorie, had come to see the kids and tell her how she'd always known Kurt was an asshole. She was as always wearing beige separates.

Delia sucked on her cigarette. "He'd be a problem all right."

"You know you can stay here as long as you need to."

"Great," said Delia. "I fuckin' love it here."

When she saw Pam at lunch she patted the seat next to her and gave her a sandwich.

. . .

Delia lay awake that night reviewing all the people she knew who had left her hometown of Winslow. There had been one boy who went to Albuquerque, but she couldn't remember his name. The shiny Gavel girls had moved to Texas but they wouldn't even speak to her in school, and that was when she'd had all her teeth. Finally, deep in the recesses of her memory, Delia found Fat Fay McDougherty. Fay had been huge, an outcast like Delia but in a different category. Delia was the only person in school who was nice to Fay, not because she liked her, but because all the kids Delia hated hated Fay. Delia had rescued Fay once when boys from school had pulled Fay's spandex pants down around her ankles and were screaming with cruel pleasure, showering her with derision. Several girls watched from a distance shaking their heads as if the boys were teasing a puppy. Delia walked up and hit one of the boys in the stomach. His name was Conroy. He was a bully with knock-knees and a crew cut. His powerful arms stuck out from his body and swung back and forth when he walked. In five years Conroy would be doing seven years for manslaughter but at the moment he was on the ground clutching his belly and the other boys just scattered. Fay pulled up her pants. She didn't even look at Delia, she just picked her books up off the grass and walked home, her thighs rubbing together. *I'll call her in the morning,* Delia thought. *If I can find her.*

. . .

"Shunt" rhymes with "cunt." That's not the reason Delia became the school slut, but it didn't help. Her father, Pete Shunt, was the only hippie in Winslow, Arizona. In 1971, at the age of thirty-four, he grew his sideburns long and started keeping goats and smoking grass he grew himself. He had always been hapless, a stunted, slim-hipped man who never developed a full beard and couldn't hold down a job. He smoked a lot of cigarettes—his one claim to manhood—and once read half a book by Kahlil Gibran, which blew his mind and, along with the sight of thousands of young people apparently without a care in the world marching against the war in Vietnam on the television screen, turned him into a hippie. He wanted that eternal childhood. He even let the Seventh-Day Adventists onto his property just to rap with them. He got so friendly with a couple of them that one day they brought their wives and their kids. They all drove up to the Shunt residence, a ramshackle clapboard two-story house with a crumbling porch, and tumbled out of their station wagons in their ironed jeans. Pete gave them lemonade and tried to teach one of the boys to play banjo. The women all

just sat smiling, calling gently to the clean-cut kids. Delia
watched through the screen door. She was embarrassed to
be seen because she had recently grown breasts. No one else
in class had them and they were huge. She looked freakish,
like a child with a stuffed bra. When she looked in the mirror it seemed as if there were cantaloupes growing under her
skin, stretching it like alien beings. Men in town looked at
her strangely and practically every boy in school had tried to
get her alone so they could cop a feel. Delia felt separate from
her breasts and kind of awed by them. They were magical
objects, and definitely not Seventh-Day Adventist material.
So she hovered behind the screen door watching. As the
morning wore on the men started making little suggestions
to Pete about how he might get his life in order—"I find
mowing the lawn regularly makes the paint on the house look
fresher"; or "A shave in the morning puts a spring in my day."
They had targeted Pete Shunt as a sinner worth the hard sell.
The morning climaxed with the head Adventist, a man named
Brown wearing horn-rimmed spectacles and a short-sleeved
button-down shirt and tie, saying that Pete would burn in Hell
unless he stopped smoking marijuana cigarettes and living
an unclean life. Pete suddenly started punching Mr. Brown
in the face and threw him right off the porch. The Adventists
scurried into their two station wagons and drove away. Pete

was sad for days after that because he had promised himself
he wasn't going to get so angry anymore. He used to hit his
wife occasionally and he hadn't done that in a long time. Delia
was especially nice to him that evening because she saw how
hurt he was by what he'd done. Her mother left soon after
that for her own reasons, mostly having to do with finance
and fashion. She was sick of being broke and wearing gauze
skirts and head scarves. She went out and bought herself a
beige skirt and white cowl neck and found a job in an insurance company. Delia decided to stay with her dad because
she felt he needed her.

Winslow was a small town, and though there were plenty
of hippies in Arizona they weren't in Winslow. So Delia had
to work hard to find a place for herself in school that wasn't
that of outcast. Her breasts made her a natural for slut and
so she went for that. Plus she loved kissing. The other stuff
she could take or leave; she hadn't figured out the mechan-
ics yet. By the time she was twelve she had lost her virginity
and she learned to be tough so she looked like she didn't care
what people thought. It was a great feeling being mean once
you got past the shame of it. Delia got really good at it. The
other girls were afraid of her even as they despised her. They
found her mysterious and dangerous, like a dark cave. The
boys were scared of her too, but they were drawn to her like
birds to crumbs and would swoop down on her in the halls at

school, leaning against the lockers making casual conversation, and all the while she could see their hard-ons under their corduroys. She learned to loved her power. There was a room behind the gym, a little dark hole where the mats were piled. That's where Delia did her business. The boys would come back there during classes and she would take their hard rubbery cocks in her cool hand. She loved to watch their faces as they rocked back and forth above her. They were powerless, rapt. She did it for free, it was her vocation. When she went home to the empty kitchen and made herself a peanut butter and jelly sandwich and one for her dad, who was usually crashed out in the darkened living room with the TV on, she would look back on the conquests of the day and it would perk her up. Her cute English teacher Mr. Clark even came by once claiming he wanted to help her with her book report. He took her for a ride in his car and they parked by the lake near town and without saying a word Delia reached over and put her hand on Mr. Clark's crotch. He touched her breast and let out a little moan and Delia thought with satisfaction that he had been thinking about doing that for a long time. Later he gave her a worse grade than she deserved. Delia accepted this; it was natural.

Kurt had big arms and puffy eyes. Delia married him at seventeen because he asked her. He asked her because he couldn't stand the idea of any other guy with his hands on

Delia. He wanted her all the time, thought about her all the time. Her ass especially, that beautiful, ripe ass. Delia could stop traffic with that ass. So he married it. She took Kurt's name like a slap in the face; it was Wurtzle. Just another case of Shunt luck, her father said. The name never really took for Delia. She was a Shunt; nothing would change that no matter how many checks she signed. But she did start having orgasms. Marriage gave a new meaning to sex for Delia. It was no longer only about power. They really made love in the beginning. That's what fooled Delia into dropping her guard and falling for her husband. Once Kurt felt her love for him, a violence crept into their lovemaking, a fierceness Delia found exciting at first until she felt the bite of his coldness and she realized that he had come to despise her. But by then it was too late. She loved him.

Delia gave birth to John about a year after the wedding. Everyone thought she must be miserable, stranded with a kid and a husband who hit. The girls she'd gone to school with avoided her in the grocery store as if she had something infectious. They didn't guess at her secret happiness. Deep in the night she heard John's frail cry and she went and picked up the baby from his cot, put his craving little mouth to her swollen tit, and watched as he stared into her eyes, satisfaction softening his features, his eyes rolling up in his head with complete and utter pleasure. Delia knew her little boy felt safe at those moments, absolutely and completely safe. It made her feel safe too.

. . .

The shelter was saddest for Delia at about ten P.M. when the children had all gone to bed and the women sat smoking, talking in hushed tones. A few of them were still in love. Many would go back, because they had nowhere else to go or because they believed things would improve. Delia didn't eat with the other women and their children—she sat apart with her kids. She didn't talk about her problems. She intimidated the other women with her silence. But Delia was just being careful. She didn't want to get soppy, she didn't want to make any mistakes. She was leaving. And she felt the women's pain and uncertainty like a vortex pulling her back into her own muddled thinking.

Delia tracked down Fat Fay McDougherty. Only it wasn't McDougherty anymore. It was Lundgren. Delia's mother had sold Fay's mother some car insurance and they'd kept in touch. It turned out Fay had moved to Why, Arizona. Her husband was in the fire department there. Delia dialed the number. Her hands were shaking. A woman with a smooth voice answered the phone with a singsong "Hello?"

"Fay?" said Delia.

"Yes?" said Fay.

"Fay, it's Delia Shunt."

There was a long moment of silence on the phone. Delia thought Fay was going to hang up. Then a tentative, even suspicious "Yes?"

"I know it's weird to be hearing from me but, ah . . . I'm kind of in a little trouble and I got no one to help me out. I mean I have to get out of town, and . . . I don't know how to explain this. I'm not wanted by the police or anything."

"I understand," said Fay. Her mother must have told her.

"It's okay if it's not possible but I thought maybe— maybe—I have three kids. And I thought maybe we could crash out in your basement or something for a couple weeks, just till I get a job and work stuff out."

Another long pause. *I must be out of my mind,* Delia thought. "Forget it," she said. "I'm sorry I bothered you."

"You might be able to stay in the garage . . ."

"Really?"

"I'd have to ask my husband. It wouldn't be too fancy."

"If there's a roof that's fine."

"There's a shower off the garage. Greg put it in last year."

"Great." Fay remembered the episode with the pants, Delia could hear it in her voice. She was sorry to have to re-mind her.

. . .

Delia had a hundred and fifty dollars from her mother,
and enough groceries to get them to Why with some left
over as a gift for Fay. They had to leave at four in the morning in case Kurt came sniffing around early. Once again
Winslow was awake, waiting for her. They had a nice trip.
They ate potato chips and ham sandwiches and drank a big
bottle of cola. It took four hours. At around seven they
stopped for gas. Delia got out, lodged the spout in the mouth
of the tank, and looked around her. The sky was streaked
with blue and pink; it looked like the inside of a seashell. In
the garage, there was a car suspended in the air. Beneath it
a man stood with a wrench in his hand. He looked over at
Delia's ass and sang, *"Lord have mercy, baby's got her blue
jeans on."*

Delia turned and looked at the man, surprised. It had
been her song, before she and Kurt were married. Whenever
she heard it she thought of herself.

*Down on the corner / by the traffic light
Everybody's looking / as she goes by*

Delia had forgotten what it was like to be appreciated.
It felt nice. But her expression hardened as she removed
the dripping nozzle from the tank and she didn't look up
again.

. . .

Why, Arizona, was just a dusty gas pump, a bank, and a general store with no produce, just some chips and soda and milk. It made Winslow look like a metropolis. Fay's house was near the train tracks. It was small and brown and tidy, in a short row of other small tidy houses. As they drove up Fay came lumbering out in an ironed red blouse and black stretch pants. Her hair was thin and teased up a few inches but her face was pretty, a little doll's face with round blue eyes and tiny teeth. She looked like someone had blown her up with a bicycle pump. Fay was nervous and so was Delia. The kids were very quiet. They had been warned twenty times not to misbehave.

Delia didn't know if she was supposed to hug Fay or what so she stood there and said, "Thanks."

"Come on in," purred Fay.

The place seemed miniature inside. The ceiling was very low. There was a little brown plush couch against one wall. Above it hung a framed poster of a soulful-looking bearded man with the words "Jesus is listening" written in script over his chest. On the couch, his feet not quite reaching the ground, sat Fay's husband, Greg. Greg was wearing green shorts and watching a football game on television, a large bowl of chips by his side. He had a mustache. His eyes roved over Delia's front for a split second, then he stood up and put his arm around Fay's waist. Delia killed the laugh that bubbled up from her gut by coughing. Greg was as tall as Fay but a quarter her size. Delia couldn't help imagining them naked.

"Where's your fire truck?" asked John.

"In the firehouse," said Greg. "I'll show it to you later if you want."

"He's a volunteer," said Fay. "His real job is—"

"I'm a—"

"A cat!" May called out hoarsely, squatting down on her chubby haunches, her brow furrowed.

"Her name is Candy," said Fay, walking toward the kitchen.

"Hey! Pssst!" May whispered. "Get over here you fuckin' cat." Delia shoved her daughter with her shoe. But Fay seemed not to have heard. She was calling back to Delia from the kitchen. "Greg's father owns the bank in Why. Greg is one of the officers."

Big shot, thought Delia, her eyes passing over Greg's skinny legs.

"Like football?" Greg asked John and Winslow.

"Yes sir," said John.

"No sir," said Winslow.

John sat next to Greg on the couch and Winslow clung to his mother's leg. May was pulling the cat toward her, dragging its legs along the ground. Delia peeled Winslow off her and joined Fay in the spotless kitchen. There was a plate of cookies on the table. They both sat down.

"They're adorable children," said Fay, pouring a glass of iced tea from a glass pitcher. She had shiny pink nails.

"Thanks," said Delia. Fay smiled contentedly, drumming her nails on the kitchen table.

"I felt so bad when my mother told me you were having a difficult time." Delia looked at the table. "How's your father?" Fay asked.

"He's all right. The same."

"Does he still keep—goats was it?" There was laughter in the back of Fay's throat when she said "goats." Like they were supposed to share the joke. Delia looked out the window. Indignation spread inside her, staining her cheeks red.

"He's retired," she said, absurdly. How can you retire if you don't do anything? Fay reached for a cookie and held it out to herself like a master to a dog, not moving the hand, holding the cookie toward her mouth but straining forward, craning her neck, her upper lip stretching down to cover her teeth demurely while her eyebrows shot up toward her hairline. Delia watched as Fay's mouth finally encircled the cookie, then bit down, never showing a glimmer of tooth—a parody of gentility.

"Where do you think I can look for a job?" Delia asked.

Fay chewed slowly, lips sealed tight. Her tongue darted out of the corners of her mouth, greedy for stray bits of sweet. Finally she swallowed.

"What kind of work would you care to do?" she asked.

"Any kind."

"I saw a sign at the café," said Fay, brushing a crumb from her bust.

The Next Café was a squat building just outside of town, frequented by some of the locals and people on their way to California. Nobody stopped in Why unless they needed a pee or a soda. Delia drove the hundred yards or so from Fay's place. It made her feel stronger than walking over like a vagrant. There was a man kneeling on the pavement just outside the entrance, talking into a low pay phone. He was wiry, grimy, with stringy black hair and a baseball cap on backward, grease-soaked jeans, and an orange T-shirt. He reminded her of her father. She passed him and walked into the café. The room was oblong. There were five booths upholstered in gray Naugahyde, two round Formica tables, and a curious three-sided structure off to one side. Waist high, covered in pink tiles, with the top upholstered in gray Naugahyde to match the booths, it looked like a place for a guard to sit behind, or maybe someone who dispenses information. Delia sat down in one of the booths. There were several customers—truckers and one old Indian lady with very long hair who kept wandering away from her harried husband and smiling at everyone she passed. Time and again the man got up and gently escorted his wife back to her seat. There was no waitress in evidence. After a few minutes, a pretty fifty-year-old lady with a gentle flip to her light brown hair came out of the kitchen breathlessly. Her blue cotton slacks were hiked up around her waist, revealing bare ankles, pull-on sneakers. She approached Delia's table smiling.

"How are you today?" she asked.

"I'm all right," said Delia.

"And— Oh!" The lady exclaimed, jumping slightly, and hurried over to the tiled structure. Reaching into it she retrieved a menu and handed it to Delia, who opened it for half a second, then shut it.

"Chicken salad okay?" Delia asked.

"It looks nice," said the lady. "It's my first day. I'm just working here temporarily to make a little extra cash."

"Chicken salad," said Delia.

"And anything for you to drink today?" She said it like the place was her living room.

"A Coke. Today," said Delia, taking out a cigarette and lighting it.

The lady rushed off to place her order. Just then a very tall, husky woman came out of the kitchen wearing what looked like a white polyester nurse's uniform, a paper shower cap on her head and paper slippers on both feet. She looked like she was leaving an operating room. She was met in the middle of the room by the man from the phone booth. He had a strange, loping walk.

"Don't forget," said the woman. "You have to pick me up at the hospital at nine."

"Okay, Ma," said the man. "So I'll get there like, ten, ten-thirty?" Then he laughed, a high, nervous laugh. His mother rolled her eyes. They left.

Delia was a good waitress. She worked fast, remembered everything, and frightened the customers just enough to keep them in line while inciting their lust, if they were men, and wariness, if they were women. If anyone was rude to her she spat in their food. It seemed fair. She never did it when she had a cold. The kids seemed to like it in Why. May got in trouble a few times for beating up the other kids in preschool, but they all followed her around anyway. Winslow went into first grade and got a gold star in reading. Every day in art class he made a card for his mom. John turned eleven in Why and his voice was hoarse from yelling all the time. The first day he got to school he told the coach he should be the captain of the baseball team without an election because he was the best. The coach said that wasn't fair. Two weeks later John was elected captain of the baseball team. He never talked about his father anymore. Delia tried to mention Kurt in a friendly way occasionally; after all, he was their dad. John's face would shut down as if he'd gone deaf. Fay's garage was pretty comfortable; the kids each had their own cot, even though by dawn Delia usually ended up with all three of them nestled around her like puppies on the pull-out couch. The children thought of their mother as immovable as granite, reassuringly scary, absolutely just.

On Sundays after church Fay would have a few of her girlfriends and their husbands over for some iced tea and they would sit in her dim parlor making desultory conversation listening to the racket of Delia's kids as they yelled at one another or Delia yelled at them. Through the window they watched as Delia came swaggering up to one of her kids and scooped him up, jerking another one by the elbow, trying to get them to contain themselves and stay in the garage—she didn't want to disturb Fay on her Sunday. Fay would watch her guests watching Delia. She would smile with her mouth shut at such moments and shake her head and one of her friends would say, "Fay Lundgren, you are a saint."

One day Delia walked into the garage after work and found Fay scrubbing her hot plate with an Brillo pad. The floor was wet, the mop leaning back on the wall reproachfully.

"What are you doing?" Delia asked.

"What does it look like I'm doing?" asked Fay in her light voice.

"I always do the cleaning at night," Delia said.

"I just thought I'd give you a hand. The place really needed a scrub!" It was at that moment that Delia realized that Fay hated her for the episode with the pants. She wanted to say, Don't bother trying to show you're better than me. You are. I mean, fuck, look at me. But she just walked outside and smoked until she heard Fay shut the door that led into the rest of the house.

That night Delia watched her kids sleeping. The tears finally came, sheets of them running down her face. She wasn't crying for the children—they would make it, she knew that now. Delia was crying because she had lost her power. She had always had a sense of her own strength, even when she was with Kurt. Now she lived with a cold pit of uncertainty in her stomach, sweat on her palms. She felt as if she were making all the moves of a person without actually being anyone at all. The years with Kurt had changed her and she hadn't realized it. She hadn't been paying attention. She thought she was so tough, she thought she could take anything. Now Kurt was gone, she had no one to fight, and she had to face the truth of what she was—a tattered cloth. And the worst of it was she missed him. She missed Sunday mornings cuddling under the blankets and little conversations as they watched TV. The fragments of peace that had glued their marriage together now wove themselves into a tapestry in Delia's mind, as if they had been continuous. She ached for him. But she rolled her tongue around in her mouth to the patch of gum where her teeth used to be and remembered the sight of John at eight raising his fist in the air over his two-year-old sister.

. . .

The greasy son of the short-order cook came in every day for a free lunch. His name was Mylert. After a couple of weeks Delia started serving him his grilled cheese sandwich and Coke without asking what he wanted. Mylert had a thin, twisted face with dark eyebrows and a pronounced Adam's apple. His wiry muscles were like steel rods beneath his skin; he had no spare flesh. His fingernails were always filthy, even when his hands were clean. He worked in the garage in town. One day when Delia set his plate and glass before him, he squinted up at her, his eyes sparkling mischievously.

"Hey Delia," Mylert said. "I don't guess you'd want to take a ride with me sometime." Delia smiled very slightly. "I'm a good driver," he said, laughing his thin, nervous laugh.

"Where you gonna drive me—crazy?" asked Delia, setting her fist on her hip. She wondered for a second if she could take him in a fight. *Hit him in the throat,* she thought absentmindedly.

"Yeah right. Heh, heh. I don't know, around. Could go to a movie. But that would be like a date. Heh, heh, heh."

"Pick me up after work. I get off at six." That got him. He was quiet for a moment.

"So I'll come by at like eight, eight-thirty?" That laugh again. The laugh of a manic thirteen-year-old.

What the hell am I doing, thought Delia.

He was waiting outside for her when she got off work. She climbed into his truck.

"Where you want to go?" he asked.

"I don't know, just drive."

He peeled off and drove out of town. They hit a stretch of road that ran straight for miles. It was flat red desert as far as you could see.

"Stop," she said. He stepped on the brakes and parked by the side of the road. Delia turned and looked at him. She could smell him from where she was sitting—sweat and grease and cigarettes. She grabbed at his hard cock under his work pants and almost made him come without even opening his fly. Then she watched the shock of pleasure on his face as she reached in and touched his skin. A massive truck thundered past just as he was coming. Afterward Delia started rooting around in her bag for a Kleenex to wipe her hands.

"Better get me back to my car," she said. "I've gotta feed my kids." He dropped her off at the restaurant where her car was parked.

"My mother's on nights at the hospital this week," Mylert said. He looked a little more relaxed than usual.

"Hey Mylert," Delia said. "You're not my boyfriend, okay?"

"I know that. Shit."

"So I don't need to know your mother's schedule," Delia said. She was standing outside the truck now, squinting in the harsh light.

"Yeah," said Mylert. "I just thought—"

"Stop thinking," said Delia, slamming the door. As Mylert drove off, she banged on his hood and, with a friendly wave, got into her hot Toyota and turned on the ignition. The radio was on. "Baby's got her blue jeans, Baby's got her blue jeans, Baby's got her blue jeans on . . ." Delia listened to the song. It was Ned McDaniel.

Up by the bus stop, and across the street,
They open up their windows, to take a peek
As she goes walkin', walkin' like a rolling stone
Heaven help us, baby's got her blue jeans on . . .

A thrill of power ran through Delia Shunt as she sat in her car watching the sun go down over Why, Arizona.

"I'm back," she said to herself, putting the car in gear. "I'm fuckin' back."

Louisa

I

Louisa Carlo was peering out the window of her parents' cramped attic, looking down at her father, Derk Carlo, who was barbecuing hamburgers on the lawn below her. Derk wasn't moving. He was just watching the burgers. Now Louisa saw her tiny blond mother, Penny, walk outside with a plate of sliced onions and tomatoes and hamburger buns. Penny set the plate on a bench next to the grill and stood next to her husband, watching the meat fry. She came up to his ribs. After a while Penny squinted up at the attic window. Louisa moved back a little so her mother wouldn't see her.

"Have you talked to her?" Penny asked.

"She's not saying much," said Derk.

"She won't talk to me."

"She's not talking."

"She might talk to you."

"She hasn't."

"Why do you think she came home?"

"Samuel, I guess."

"Oh." Penny slumped down onto the bench. "I hope she's all right."

"She'll be all right. Louisa's tough."

"Some things are just too hard for a person to take," said Penny.

"I know," said Derk, lifting a patty gently to check its underside, thinking that all the women in his family were just a little bit off.

Every morning of his life Derk Carlo had eaten three fried eggs. One of Louisa's most piercing childhood memories was of Penny frying up his eggs with five strips of bacon. Derk would sit at the table reading the paper, his massive forearm propped on the red checked tablecloth like a sleeping beast. At 8:15 he would leave for the butcher shop. Sometimes when Louisa was a kid she'd tag along. She watched transfixed as her dad sliced veal, severed chops, minced beef, and handed the neat soft white wax-paper packages over the counter to the women. Even then Louisa could tell they wanted him. The ladies of Dutchess County swarmed into Carlo Meats like hornets, dressed to the nines, just to have a few sweet words with that terse bull of a butcher. Derk was six-foot-five and his white apron seemed to stretch on forever over the vast expanse of his chest. Yet he never seemed to notice the women's feverish signaling. The only concession he made to their powers was an extra chop in the wax paper now and then. "Don't start anything you can't finish" was one of Derk's favorite maxims. And the truth was he loved his wife.

Penny was a natural towhead. She had wide hips, a slender waist, a lisp, and pockmarked skin. Her cheeks were slightly fuzzy, like a peach, which made her seem a little bit blurry. Life was hard for Penny. She was always wondering if she had done the wrong thing and could berate herself for weeks if a piecrust had gone tough for company. Her own father was a bully, a big man in town who used his daughter's goodwill endlessly, asking her to make dinners for him and her brother years after she'd been married, calling her to pick him up from the golf course, getting her to do his shopping. Penny was a doormat. She was a devoted and perky mother, always present at sports events even though Louisa was a hopelessly indifferent athlete. At a softball game once Penny couldn't see Louisa anywhere, not even at her usual spot on the bench, so she went wandering around looking for her as the game ambled on. She finally found her fair, fragile daughter behind the backstop, making mud pies and singing to herself.

When Louisa was twelve Penny started changing. She sank into reveries and sighed a lot. On rainy afternoons Louisa would hover uneasily at the door as her mother sat in the darkened living room listening to Peggy Lee. "Is that all there

is to a fire?" Louisa guessed that Penny's sadness had something to do with the missing baby. Louisa had been born a
twin. Her brother Seth lived two days. He never even opened
his eyes. Watching her mother sit so still in there, Louisa's
cheeks went hot with shame. Sometimes in the night she
dreamed that she had killed her brother in Penny's cramped
womb; there wasn't enough blood and bone for both of them
so she reached into her brother's chest and took out his heart.
He just looked at her, mute and helpless, as if he were giving
himself up. Louisa knew they were divided—good baby, bad
baby. Her guilt had been written in blood on her strong shiny
body as the nurses rushed her other self away in a hush.
Louisa knew just what Seth would have been like. He would
have been funny and sweet. He would have given great advice. He would never have let anyone hurt Penny, especially
not Louisa. When Louisa was growing up she used to play
with her brother all the time. She would tell him everything,
even boss him around. The day Penny found her making mud
pies behind the backstop she was playing with Seth. He was
sprinkling sand on the pies like brown sugar.

Louisa knew Seth still pulled at her mother's memory
even though nobody in the house ever mentioned him. The
weeks went by and Penny stayed sad. When Derk came home
dinner was frozen pizza or frozen lasagna or Hamburger
Helper. Penny was imploding.

One day she started throwing pots in Mrs. Talbot's Intro-
duction to Clay at the Delton Art Association. Her first pots
were misshapen, lumpen, even pathetic. Louisa would look at
them lined up on the windowsill as she ate her cereal in the
morning and they worried her. She was protective of Penny.
But one day Penny had a breakthrough. She brought home the
evidence in a cake box and let it sit ominously on the kitchen
table for hours before revealing it. She wanted Derk to be
home. At the appointed time Derk and Louisa stood at the
table, each dreading the revelation of another monstrosity.

. . .

It was an ashtray. It was incredible. There were mermaids
perched around the edge—little blond middle-aged women
with pendulous, cucumberlike breasts, fluorescent pink tails,
and double chins. The inside of the ashtray was glazed cer-
ulean blue and vibrated against the pink of the fishtails. There
were extravagant flowers with their petals opened suggestively on each corner and—this is what fascinated Louisa most
of all—four little pink tongues for the cigarettes. You could
see the taste buds. Louisa and Derk just stood staring at it
for a very long time. Penny was staring at it too. She had a
dreamy expression on her soft fuzzy face.

Penny kept throwing pots and they continued to be splen-
didly horrible. Louisa would await each new creation with

excitement and a spike of dread. Sometimes she imagined that her mother had disappeared and an actress had taken her place. The proof was in the pots; her real mother would not make pots like this. Within a year Penny was offered a show at the Delton Art Association. She was ecstatic and terrified. It was a triumph; she sold every piece. Delton was an old farming town sprinkled with people who actually lived in Manhattan, or who might as well have. The women went mad for Penny's stuff. It was so hilarious. And though their appreciation was ironic, it was genuine—they felt they had discovered an idiot savant. Suddenly Penny and Derk were being invited to a whole new class of house. The rich bohemians welcomed them like a circus act.

. . .

The first time Louisa was invited along to one of these occasions, it was at Felicia French's house. Ms. French was a historical novelist in her forties with sharp features and blond ringlets. As the Carlos drove up to the old farmhouse, a peacock walked across the driveway and started pecking under the tires of the Frenches' Mercedes.

Inside, the walls were covered in abstract paintings, the floors in Oriental rugs. The furniture was brown and low and old. Felicia French was very tall, with sharp elbows and knees. She perched herself on the arm of Derk's chair like an underfed condor and began to explain to him in urgent, broken sentences that she was working on a book about a cruel eighteenth-century duke who pinned virgins to the wall with hat pins. At least that's what Louisa thought she heard her say. Derk listened to Ms. French's fervent description as he looked out the window with his dead-eyed gaze, sipping his whiskey sour. When she finally stopped, breathless, Derk paused for a moment. Then he said, flatly, "Sounds like quite a job." Ms. French laughed, a high, girlish laugh. Then she started asking him about the subtleties of meat.

Ms. French's husband, Bill, was a small, quiet man with a glossy brown mustache. He wrote novellas. He was listening to Herbert Breem, the famous painter, with a look of exaggerated interest on his kindly face. Mr. Breem, a stout man in his fifties with a florid complexion and very small feet, was speaking in a booming voice. "Oh yes," he said. "I've got a show on up in Boston at the moment. The one in New York closed last week. Marvelous notices. Did you see the *Times* review?"

"No," said Mr. French apologetically. "We just skim the paper in the summer. Just to be sure we haven't started another war or anything."

"Well, Epstein came 'round!"

"That's fantastic—Epstein!" said Mr. French.

"His review was marvelous," said Breem's distracted wife, Martha, in a gravelly, flat midwestern voice as she popped a bit of smoked salmon into her slash of a mouth. "Epstein said Herb was turning into an abstract icon."

"Well!" said Mr. French eagerly. "Must be hard to wait in line at the Laundromat with reviews like that, huh?" Mr. French's gelatinous quip missed Breem entirely and landed with a splat at the feet of Melodie Simms, the young feminist whose instant incendiary classic, (*You Are*), was in its fifth week on the *New York Times* best-seller list. Ms. Simms was reclining on the flaking leather couch in a trim black velvet pantsuit, drinking a martini, and smiling at Mr. French's remark. Her fine brown hair swirled about her small head like dandelion fuzz and her slightly bulging gray eyes stared about her hungrily. Louisa recognized Ms. Simms from her book jacket. (*You Are*) was presently being circulated in Louisa's school among the girls like a copy of *Hustler*. Louisa had read only a few paragraphs, looking over Sexy Betsy Lape's shoulder (Betsy had filched it from her older sister Amelia). It seemed to be about a woman who travels around looking for anonymous love. She wants only strangers. She sees a guy on a train and undoes his fly, doesn't even ask him his name. Louisa couldn't believe Melodie Simms was sitting right in front of her. It made her blush.

Mr. Breem continued, "Then I have a show in Munich in November and in January it's . . ." he looked to his wife.

"Gratz," said Martha, her mouth clotted with food.

"Right." One of Breem's paintings was hanging right over his head, and he looked up at it for a moment, craning his neck, absorbed as if seeing for the first time. It was a vast canvas which was almost entirely maroon but for a few brushy fuchsia marks that floated in its bland expanse like guppies in an empty shark tank.

The guest of honor was a famous Russian writer who had been in prison for a long time but seemed, to Louisa, to have eaten quite a lot during his incarceration. He had a very long beard with bits of chopped chicken liver in it. His wife was a poet. She had misty, kohl-blackened eyes and bangs and to-bacco stains on her teeth. She looked like she was going to cry all evening, but she never managed. Louisa kept an eye on Penny from across the room, anxious that she be all right in this company. Her mother was wearing a hot-pink hostess suit that had a matching hat. Louisa was grateful that she'd left the hat in the car. She knew Penny was desperately shy but even more desperate for approval. Her tiny voice barely squeaked out of her and she never stopped smiling. Louisa watched as Ms. French approached Penny, towering and bony in a Bedouin wedding dress, looking as if she'd dressed to match the carpet. Automatically Louisa moved to her mother's side, sensing her unease.

"Your pots—" said Ms. French, "—so deeply funny and weirdly erotic and—I just—can't get enough of them!" Penny gasped slightly and let out a little stifled high-pitched laugh. Louisa saw Ms. French flick an amused glance at Martha Breem. Now Bryna Doyle, a neighbor of Penny's—her husband had gone to Delton High with Derk—came round with a glass of white wine on a tray. Penny grabbed at it, embarrassed to be served by a friend, wanting to get the moment over with.

"Hi, Mrs. Doyle," said Louisa. "Hello, Louisa," said Mrs. Doyle. Penny gulped at the wine, spilling a little on her front. "Thank you—thank you—" she said. Louisa watched her, surprised. Penny usually drank milk with her supper. After a few sips her cheeks flushed slightly and her shoulders relaxed. Bryna Doyle, a tall, doughy woman, shuffled away in her flats, casting a glance at a candy dish of Penny's on the piano. It was shaped like a mouth and lined with little pearly teeth. Louisa saw Bryna roll her eyes.

It was eight o'clock. Glancing out the window, Louisa saw several naked men assembling on the lawn. Her first instinct was to shield her mother's eyes.

"Oh here they are!" Bill French said. Everyone in the party gathered at the picture window to have a look. The naked men started picking each other up and twirling each other around in the golden light, their purple shadows dancing on the grass. One sprang off another's thighs and vaulted through the air. It looked like he was flying. The Frenches' peacock stalked majestically past the dancers. Everybody laughed.

"My God, Felicia, did you rehearse the *bird?*" somebody asked.

"Of course, darling. God is in the details!" Ms. French laughed, her eyes flitting over to Derk.

Suddenly a naked woman popped up in the midst of the men. She had black hair to her waist and tiny breasts. The men threw her around like a doll stuffed with straw. "She's marvelous," said Mr. Breem. Penny and Louisa remained frozen on the couch during the performance but they could see out the window perfectly well, between Mr. Breem's corduroy jacket and Ms. French's Bedouin wedding dress. Mrs. Doyle came by again with the wine and Penny took another glass. The dancers went running off as if they had suddenly realized they didn't have any clothes on. There was scattered clapping, then Penny let out a sudden, hysterical titter and clamped her hand over her mouth. Everyone looked at her. Her eyes were glassy and she was pale. She smiled vaguely and said with her slight lisp, "I've never seen a man naked before. Except for Derk."

The moment of silence that followed filled Louisa with dread. Melodie Simms leaned forward slightly in her seat, intrigued.

"Damn," said Derk. "Now she knows what's out there." Everyone laughed, automatically. Whatever Derk said, you

took it the way he meant you to. His salt-of-the-earth presence was like a stamp of authenticity on his wife's fuzzy little
forehead. No quotation marks on Penny. She was the real
thing. Felicia French even clapped her hands in delight—
she was so happy to have discovered the Carlos.

Louisa was fascinated by the rich bohemians. They never
seemed embarrassed or awkward, they were always glib. She
called them the raincoat people because everything just rolled
right off their shoulders. By the time everyone sat down to
dinner, the dancers had joined the party. One of the men kept
looking at Louisa over the dinner table. He was about twenty,
with light brown hair and full lips. His name was Peter. He
seemed shy but he asked her name. Louisa pretended to
herself that he was her brother, and imagined going off to a
secret room with him to whisper about what was going on.
Then she imagined he wasn't her brother, and they went into
the secret room and kissed.

Penny kept drinking, and her face began to change; her
features coarsened, her fair cheeks were mottled with red.
She had shrugged off her modesty like a cape and was giggling suggestively with Mr. Breem, who was teasing her. She
was turning into somebody else. Louisa kept looking at Derk,
as if for help, but he didn't seem to notice.

At one point Melodie Simms leaned over Bill French to
ask Louisa, "How old are you?"

"Fourteen and a half," said Louisa.

Melodie screamed a laugh across the table at Felicia French. Louisa jumped in her chair.

"I love it when they include the half year, so they seem older!" Melodie said. Then she turned back to Louisa. "Honey, if only you knew what we know—you'd be wishing you were twelve." Everybody laughed, including Penny. Her teeth were stained with wine.

Before dessert, the Russian exile took out a hefty manuscript and began to read aloud melodiously in Russian while everyone listened, glassy-eyed. Louisa excused herself and wandered into the empty living room. Mr. Breem's painting looked different now. It was a pulsing, vast, empty field of red, lonely as the bottom of the sea. Louisa stared at it for a long time until she began to feel afraid. As if a creature might crash out of that deep and devour her.

When the evening was over Louisa was so angry at Penny she couldn't look her in the face. Her skin burned where her mother brushed against it as she followed Derk unsteadily to the car. It felt as if Penny had left her and a monstrous phantom had stepped into her skin. Louisa hated this simulacrum as much as she adored her mother. But all she could do was wait till morning, till the real Penny would come into her room all smiley and ready for a walk in the woods if it was a weekend or making jam or just reading together all

curled up near the bay window on a rainy day. Louisa loved
her mother's smell.

. . .

Penny's success came to a climax when she was invited
to participate in a show of "Outsider Art" in Manhattan. Her
four-foot-high paperweight was displayed between a painting of twin poodles by a schizophrenic man and a tongue-
depressor sculpture by a housewife from Dubuque. The
paperweight was sold to a man from Geneva who owned a
collection of porcelain figurines made by eighteenth-century
midgets. Though short, Penny did not fit into this category.
The collector said that her paperweight, which was encrusted
with angels and little brown mice, was so divine that it de-
fied all categories. Louisa was fascinated by the art of pretend liking. You had to know something was horrible and like
it as a joke, but the thing had to give you real pleasure at the
same time. The trick was to remember to laugh at it inside.
Otherwise you were just a chump who loved shitty stuff.
Penny was so nervous at the opening that she could barely
stand. Louisa spent most of the night holding her elbow.
Penny didn't get drunk that night because Louisa kept getting her Cokes. Penny drank at home now. She drank to relax.
She drank to celebrate. She drank to console herself. Bit by
bit Louisa was turning away from her. When Penny spoke to

her Louisa was surly and mean. Penny was bewildered. Derk said it was because Louisa was a teenager.

But Louisa didn't look like a teenager. At sixteen she looked thirteen. She hadn't gotten her period and the doctor was talking about giving her hormones. She would stand in front of the mirror for ages staring at her body, trying to discern the slightest change.

In March of the following year Penny had another show at the Delton Art Association. At the opening people kept whispering to one another as if there were a corpse in the next room. Penny had remembered her religion. Mopey brown Virgins stooped over muddy lakes staring at their doleful reflections. Terriers on their hind legs held the Book of Revelations between their teeth. Louisa stood near the door listening to what people were saying as they left. She heard Felicia French say to Martha Breem: "Sad ashtrays just aren't my idea of a good buy."

At the end of the opening Penny was standing alone in the corner, still smiling, with tears in her eyes. She hadn't sold one piece. Derk went over and patted her head, his version of a hug.

The rich bohemians stopped inviting them over. Penny kept calling the hostesses asking them to dinner, thinking surely her exclusion was just a sin of omission. But it wasn't. The joke of Penny and her pots had run its course. In the evenings Penny's eyes would blink very slowly as she stared out the window at the darkening sky, drunk, while Derk ate his steak, breathing noisily through his nose. Louisa sat staring at her plate, rigid as a stone.

II

Louisa went to art school at seventeen filled with rage. She wanted to avenge her mother. Within a week of leaving home the blood ran down her legs in little rivulets and pooled at her feet, shiny as rubies.

She met Sam in first-year life-drawing class. The model was a hugely fat man and Louisa was enjoying the session tremendously—she loved drawing flesh. Sam was set up behind her. He was fascinated by the way she drew; she barely looked at the paper. She just seemed to know where her charcoal was on the page. When class was over she walked away from her easel, leaving her drawing up, and started down the hall to the elevator.

"Hey, ah, excuse me—"

Louisa turned around. A slender young man wearing baggy canvas trousers and round spectacles was waving to her from the classroom door.

"You forgot your drawing," he said.

"Oh," said Louisa, hurrying back, the blood rushing to her cheeks. "Jesus. Sorry." She hated the idea of the drawing being scrutinized; it was a mess. She glanced at Sam as she passed him. He had a kind, round, serious face with brown eyes, dark brows, and curly chestnut hair. Sam watched Louisa as she tore the drawing off the stand and hurried out of the room again.

He kept an eye out for her after that, watching her drift through her first three love affairs, all of them students who approached her and were accepted rather than chosen. It took too much effort to move away. Louisa lived to paint. Often when Sam came into the art building for his first class, she was still in her studio. She'd been there all night. Sometimes he'd bring her donuts.

. . .

Sam fell in love with Louisa by watching her live. Desire came last.

. . .

She was tiny—just five feet. Her light blond hair fell in a tangled veil to her thighs. Her hands and feet were small as a child's. She had a crooked little face, a small mouth, a little birthmark between her eyebrows. Her eyes were the color of a muddy pond. Her breasts were small and pudgy, with fat aureoles and inverted nipples. Her tummy was soft and she had an arch in her back. Her legs were sturdy but not defined. Sam couldn't decide if she was ugly or beautiful.

He finally decided she was beautiful and left a note
tucked into her metal drawing stand:

> *She is handsome, she is pretty*
> *She is the girl of the golden city*
> *She goes courting one, two, three—*
> *Please and tell me, who is she?*

She read the note and scanned the room. Sam was looking at her. He blushed.

. . .

They were twenty in New York City and they were a
golden couple. They danced and they made fun of themselves
and of each other and they were like lusty children. They
played and played and Louisa found to her delight that wher-
ever her mind went Sam could follow, and then go further,
and she would follow. Sam's paintings were abstract, precise,
and gorgeous. He knew color. He knew how to make a square
of red feel like rain clouds, or happiness, or sex. Louisa
watched as Sam dragged a brush loaded with gray alongside
a mass of reddish orange. The edge where the two colors met
vibrated; it was violent. When he surrounded the same red
with violet, the two colors radiated tranquillity. Through Sam,
Louisa entered a new domain. She began to learn her craft

more deeply and more humbly. She expected more from herself. And he could always make her laugh. Three years went
by and they finished art school. Sam went to graduate school
right away. They moved into an Italian neighborhood in
Queens, near the school. The old women sat outside the
buildings in lawn chairs watching people go by. Sam and
Louisa got their own lawn chairs and sat with the old ladies.
Their apartment was spacious and cheap, with a great old pink
dinette set in the kitchen and a pressed-tin ceiling. They each
had a room to use as a studio. Louisa would paint all morning and Sam would come home at lunch. Louisa would cook
some odd combination of foods—spinach leaves wrapped
around mashed plantains, for example—and they would sit
down to an unsatisfactory but jolly little meal. Then they'd
both paint. At night some of their friends from art school
would come by for dinner if Louisa wasn't waiting tables at
the bar down the street. There were hardly any lights in the
apartment and they had to hold candles over the stove to see
the food they were cooking. By the time the pasta was ready
everyone was drunk on cheap Hungarian wine. Louisa started
having the same dream over and over: She dreamed she was
baby-sitting for her brother Seth. She gave him a bath and his
limbs started coming off in the water. They had turned to plastic. Louisa was desperate, trying to put him back together. But
there was nothing left. She began to paint from her dream.

. . .

One day Louisa realized that she and Sam hadn't made love in a month. Another month went by and they didn't make love, and then another. They would just sort of forget about it. Louisa was happiest being like a child with Sam, playing like a child, speaking like a child. She'd stopped feeling any desire at all. One night she dreamed that Seth entered Sam like a viper as he slept, crawling from Louisa's mouth into his ear.

. . .

Little things about Louisa that had amused Sam before began to irritate him. He would find her notebooks in the refrigerator, sandwiches on the radiator, dust balls the size of rats on the stairs. Her absent mindedness began to infuriate him. Louisa never understood what the problem was. She hated being berated. Another year went by; they made love once. Louisa decided she should get her own place and started to wonder if maybe she was a lesbian.

. . .

Olive Blackman had an aquiline nose and a bush the size of a hedgehog. She was a waitress at the alternative muffin shop near Louisa's new studio in Chinatown. Louisa loved napping between Olive's sizable breasts but would do anything to avoid performing oral sex, suggesting one activity after another—movies, theater, charades. Eventually she faced the fact that she wasn't a lesbian and started getting her muffins someplace else.

. . .

Bruno was a painter. He had straight black hair that hung past his shoulders and the most stunning pelvis, which he always managed to leave bare. He roomed with a few other artists in a crack-infested building on the Lower East Side. The group lived entirely ironically. They listened to Guns N' Roses ironically, performing elaborate air guitar sequences that they didn't really mean. They ate ironic snacks: Hostess Twinkies with Slim Jims shoved through the center. They spoke endlessly about the pop culture of their childhoods: "The United States loses the Vietnam War; Greg Brady gets a perm." They jeered at everything—other painters, rich people, crack heads, politicians, newscasters, tampon commercials, pop stars, people with aquariums. Everything but Warhol. Bruno's paintings were a skillful cross between Otto Dix and mall art.

Irony made Louisa feel strong. It was a pleasure that went back to her childhood, to the raincoat people and the art of pretend liking. Now she really knew how to pretend-like. She was an expert and could have blown that Swiss collector of eighteenth-century midget porcelain out of the water. Even so, Louisa always felt like a stranger in the group; the snide way of life wasn't natural to her and she was often at the brink of tears in the company of her new friends. But she enjoyed the loud music, the filterless cigarettes, the beer. And the sex. Louisa and Bruno made love all the time—in his studio, in her studio, in other people's studios, in bathrooms, subways, drugstores. If they went longer than three days without it Louisa would become jittery and cry easily. Bruno fell in love with her and became shockingly sentimental. Louisa kept thinking that any day now she was going to fall in love with him.

Once or twice a month during this period she and Sam would get together, at their old place or in a restaurant. They would talk and laugh but he always ended up putting her into a cab crying, filled with loss and regret. She would watch him through the window as the cab drove off. He'd stand there until he couldn't see her anymore.

One day she went to a dingy used-book store on Eighteenth Street with Bruno. They often wandered around the city looking for places to fool around, and Louisa needed something to read. They moved through the self-help section slowly, apparently ignoring each other as they fed the erotic nimbus that would build up and enfold them. Eventually, wandering through the maze of shelves, they came to a dead end, a little room of books piled six feet high with titles like *Jewish Recipes and Their Relation to the Talmud,* or *Dinah Shore: The Woman with the Voice.* It was a book graveyard. Louisa looked over at Bruno. He was flipping through a hardback. Eventually he looked up and came over to her. She was wearing a long battered raincoat. He slipped his hands around her waist and kissed her. His hand wrestled its way into her jeans. Louisa rested her head on his shoulder and looked around. She felt sorry for the spurned books. Their absurd titles stared out at her like the sad hopeful eyes of impounded dogs waiting for new masters. She shut her eyes and imagined that she was at the pound to rescue a stray and Bruno was the handsome young attendant who just couldn't keep his hands off her. Afterward, she chose two books—a 1974 manual on how to save your marriage through breath therapy, and a book about breeding beagles.

The line for the register was long and Louisa stood waiting alone while Bruno browsed in the art section. When it came her turn to pay, Louisa looked up and saw someone she recognized. It was Miles Coburn! Louisa had lost her virginity to Miles on a camp bed in art school when she was seventeen. He left her three weeks later for a plump-fronted photo-realist named Phyllis.

"Louisa?" he said. They exchanged a few awkward words and she left with Bruno. But later she found herself curious about Miles and, when Bruno went home, she circled back to the bookstore. It was about six o'clock and Miles was just getting off work. They went to a bar. It felt odd and exciting seeing him again, as if she were talking to a ghost. Their affair had happened so long ago—before Sam, even. Apparently Phyllis, the realist, was his for five long years until he left her for a Japanese hypochondriac named Yoshi who had him believing she had irritable bowel syndrome until it turned out she was just cracked. He explained all this to Louisa with a mumbled, James Dean–like delivery. Miles had a crooked nose and dirty-blond hair and always walked like he was a little bit drunk. Now he was sitting underneath a gleaming stuffed swordfish with a half-finished ginger ale in front of him. He had fallen silent and was looking out the window at passersby.

"Are you painting?" she asked.

"When I can."

Louisa remembered his murky, ineffectual nudes, but she pushed the thought from her mind, feeling a tug deep inside, as if a dog was dragging a forgotten bone from the ground. She couldn't help herself; she had to seduce him. They talked all night. "I can't believe I let you go," he said. She left Bruno a week later with the zeal of a convert. For the next three weeks she and Miles went everywhere together. When they were apart they spent hours on the phone.

They slept locked in each other's arms. Louisa could smell
her innocence on his skin. It felt like fate.

Miles lived way uptown so they always stayed in Louisa's
studio. She kept meaning to go see his paintings, but a month
passed and still she hadn't gone. Finally they set the date. As
she sat wedged into the crowded A train, a dull ache of anxiety spread in her chest. She didn't know why she was so nervous. It took her several minutes to notice the man standing
over her, hanging by a hand strap, staring at her. When she
felt his gaze and looked up, for a split second she thought he
was attractive in a brutish sort of way. Then she saw that he
was crazy. He was thickset, with a massive jaw and dense
brown hair, black sunglasses and a torn gray shirt, portable
headphones around his filthy neck. He looked away from
Louisa, down the line of other passengers, and started rubbing his crotch. Louisa was frightened. Next to her was an
Orthodox Jew in his thirties with pale skin and delicate nostrils, ringlets tucked behind his ears. His eyes met hers and
he whispered, "That man is very sick,"

"Yup," said Louisa, keeping her cool. What was she going
to do, start hanging on to the man's elbow? Ask him to walk
her to her boyfriend's house?

"I think," he said, "maybe you should get off." She smiled
at him a little. He seemed so decent. He seemed like a man

who would never hurt anyone, who was nice to his wife. He
probably had seven children. He lived by the rules, he had
rules! Louisa was racked by a sudden, acute yearning for an
orderly life. The train stopped. She got up and rushed out
the door. She ran the fifteen blocks to Miles's building. When
he opened the door she hugged him for a long time. He
stroked her head. She wished that they had already been
married for years and that their children were playing outside the farmhouse. She wished for a bowl of spaghetti in front
of the TV. She turned to see the apartment.

It was a sunny little room with a spider plant in the window and pudgy, comfortable furniture. There were several
paintings on the walls. They were academic-style setups: nude
woman reclining on couch, nude woman perched on chair,
nude woman reading the paper. Louisa recognized the deft
but vague use of paint from Miles's paintings in art school—
a cunning ocher splotch here is the cat; mix up a dark
almost-black (Thalo Green, Ultramarine Blue, and Alizarine
Crimson, in equal proportions), draw the number-five
natural-bristle brush across just so, and you have a rich shadow
under the couch; an orange-pink dollop is the face. They were
competent and dull. She felt like weeping. Miles offered her
herbal tea. Louisa sat under the spider plant. He touched her
hand, concerned. "Are you all right?" he asked. She smiled reassuringly. But she didn't recognize him anymore. Suddenly

he seemed as predictable and earnest as his paintings. "I just—where's the bathroom?" He showed her. She went in, locked the door, sat on the edge of the bathtub, and sobbed.

Louisa didn't have the heart to end it with Miles. She just carried her extinguished emotion around like a dead body until finally the weight of it stilled her entirely and she took to her bed, telling Miles she couldn't see him for a while because she didn't feel well. After a couple of weeks she fell into an animated conversation in the hallway with her next-door neighbor, a married guy named Ed. Ed was writing a novel and worked in construction. He was medium height, medium build, with a thicket of black hair cropped close to his head and a penis shaped like a toadstool—but Louisa didn't know that yet. She liked him mainly because he always had white dust on his work boots. She didn't want to read his novel. Three days later Ed leaned on Louisa's bell at one o'clock in the morning. "Who is it?" she asked, her voice broken with sleep and apprehension. "Ed. Ed Shriver. If this is a bad—" She opened the door for him and turned back toward her bed without a word. Uncertain what to do, Ed followed her. Louisa threw herself onto the mattress on the floor and curled up under the tangle of sheets and blankets, her back to him. After a few awkward seconds Ed shrugged, took off his pants, and lay down next to her. There were no curtains on the windows and the night glow

of the city illuminated the empty loft. Louisa's wooden armchair stood in the middle of the room, facing a large obscured painting. A drunk man was talking out on the street.
He was making a point very loudly. It sounded like he was
in her bathroom. He was a bore. Louisa knew the type. She
hated sleeping by herself. She was glad Ed had shown up.
She let him turn her around and kiss her. At about eight in
the morning, with the white light bleaching out the loft
windows and the noise of Canal Street echoing in the empty
room, Louisa got up, still without looking at the man in her
bed, and started to make coffee. Ed propped himself up on
one elbow and watched. There were paintings on the walls
and stacked in corners. Some of the paintings had middle-
aged mermaids in them. Others were of twins. There was a
phone on the floor surrounded by several crushed Coke
cans. Louisa was wearing a torn yellow silk kimono that had
been made for a small child; it hung from her narrow shoulders like rags, her blond hair in a tangle down her back. She
opened the refrigerator. It was bare but for a wilted bunch
of broccoli and a small container of heavy cream, which she
removed and put on the lone chair. Then she looked over
at the bed. "You're up," she said.

"Mmhm," he said. The coffee boiled and sputtered to the
top of the pot.

"Why are you here, anyway?" she asked.

"I was having a terrible night, I thought we could talk," he said.

"Oh," she said, laughing. "Well I guess we can talk now. What happened to your wife, anyway?"

"I don't know. Something. She left me."

"She'll probably come back."

"I don't think so." He looked pathetic.

"Boy, I feel really sorry for your next girlfriend," she said, "coming after a wife." She brought him his coffee and sat down on the bed.

"Doesn't it get you down, living like this?" he asked.

"What do you mean, the furniture? I'm getting chairs."

"No. I mean—the whole thing."

"I don't really notice."

"What are you doing today?" he asked.

Louisa shrugged. "Working," she said.

They slept together on and off after that, whenever they happened to meet in the hallway or he rang the bell, until one day she stopped answering the door. But by that time she was already seeing a stock analyst named Bernard.

Timothy was a playwright. Adam was a painter. Simon was a painter. Felix was a photographer. Jesse was a businessman. She met them in other people's apartments, in galleries, cafés, and would wander off and start a relationship. But once they weren't strangers anymore, the spell always broke.

And the process of disenchantment was speeding up. Louisa always left bewildered by her own alienation, holding a tattered bag of endearments she had used too many times.

She began to think there was something wrong with her and went to a therapist, a chubby Jungian named Zwick who wore tight corduroy pants so his fat balls were wedged in there, and during all Louisa's sessions beneath her conscious thoughts she kept thinking of ways to free this man's balls. Eventually she just stopped showing up.

It had been five years since Louisa moved out of the apartment in Queens. She was twenty-eight. One morning she and Sam were having breakfast in a coffee shop near her studio. They were both tired. Sam was going out with a girl who worked at *Marriage Now* magazine. Louisa leaned her head against the wall and looked at him. He looked back at her and smiled a sad little smile. Louisa noticed for the first time that an expression of disappointment was settling into Sam's features. She put her hand out and he held it.

"Do you love me?" she asked.

"Yes."

"More than anyone else?"

"Yes."

"Let's move back in together. At least then we'll know for sure."

Sam was ambivalent but he needed to know too. They managed to find a place with a three-month lease for their experiment. It was crammed with other people's stuff. After a couple of weeks of kidding around and playing house like the old days, they made the effort of lying naked beside each other in candlelight, staring intently into each others' eyes, until they both burst into fits of crazy laughter at the idea of having sex. It just wasn't there. Louisa felt strangely relieved. The transformation was complete. They were related.

III

One night Louisa went to a friend's house alone for a party. Naked bulbs in the ceiling threw harsh white light on some faces; others moved in pools of darkness. There was jazz playing. As she walked through the living room to drop her coat on the bed, Louisa noticed a stranger leaning against the cluttered counter in the kitchen speaking to someone she couldn't see. The stranger was tall and hunched, uneasy in his body, slightly overweight. His thick greasy black hair hung over one eye and he moved it away with a pale slender hand. There was paint on his pants.

"Who is that?" Louisa asked her friend Susan, who had come over to her with a beer. Susan looked over at the kitchen.

"That's Samuel Shapiro. He's a painter. He's really good."

They had coffee the following week. Samuel Shapiro had an oddly formal manner. He couldn't find a gallery even though everyone who knew his work thought he was a genius. He made a point of mentioning that his father collected garbage for a living. Louisa couldn't wait to get away from him. She didn't think she'd see him again. But he called and she went to his studio. She was curious to see his work. He lived on Fourteenth and Tenth. Louisa descended the dank stairs to the basement. Samuel Shapiro opened the door and bowed slightly in greeting. Louisa started to laugh at this but then she didn't. She followed him down the short, dimly lit hallway. The buzz of fluorescent lights sounded like insects. There was a smell in the air—Louisa couldn't quite place it— that was both alluring and disgusting, a full, familiar aroma. Then she came into the room. The paintings were enormous. They filled every inch of wall space. Louisa walked in trying to orient herself, trying to see them one by one in the greenish light. They were more drawings than paintings—fine red scratch marks on the white canvas. Each painting was a chapter in a story. A young woman was in a wedding veil in one picture; in the next her throat was being slashed. Red paint was smeared all over the canvas. It looked like real blood. The image was spare and frightening. This guy was really good.

"It's the story of the sacrifice of Iphigenia. Do you know it?"

"I remember it vaguely. Her father sacrificed her . . ."

"Her father Agamemnon sacrificed her so the wind would blow and the ships could sail for Troy and start the Trojan War."

"Helen of Troy," she said. "What a pain in the ass." Samuel laughed, a short, unwilling little laugh. Louisa walked around the room. The paintings were cruel and grand. He offered her a beer. She accepted. She walked up behind him as he reached into the refrigerator and saw inside several white plastic containers full of liquid. Samuel saw her looking, reached in, and took out one of the containers, peeling back the lid. It was blood. "I get it from the slaughterhouse on Forty-eighth Street," he said. Louisa made a face as she peered into the container. She looked back up at the blood-stained canvases. Christ.

"How do you get it thick enough to paint with?" she asked.

"I mix it with acrylic primer." She looked up at Samuel. His black eyes, rimmed with purplish shadows, stared into her, unblinking. He was looking at her as if he knew something about her, something secret. A part of her wanted to flee, to run down the stairs and get this smell of death out of her nose. But she felt the strength drain out of her. She was going to stick around, she could tell.

His torso was fat and hairy but his limbs were delicate as a girl's. His hair smelled of smoke and musk. His eyes were filled with suffering. He tied her wrists behind her back. He whispered insulting things into her ear and they dripped into her brain like poison that leaked from between her legs and betrayed what she wanted. She'd finally found out the truth about herself. He would ask for a glass of water and when she got up to fetch it for him he would snap his fingers and say, "Slave!" He was kidding but he would do it again and again. She got very angry but she couldn't throw him out. For the first time since Sam she felt like she belonged to somebody, linked. Sam/Samuel: it seemed strangely perfect that they shared a name. She wanted to marry him. He lacerated her work:

"You know how to paint. But . . . this innocence shit. I don't believe it. It's soft. You're too soft on yourself. You've got everyone telling you how cute you are and they confuse you with your work. They're girl paintings." Louisa railed feebly against his diatribes; in her heart she believed she might not be any good. When it turned out that Ulrich Wemmer, a rising Berlin artist, had been painting in blood for a decade, Samuel was inconsolable. It totally screwed up his chances. And anyway he put the gallery people off when they came to his studio for visits. He became stilted, overly polite yet cold. They felt his disdain and his anger. He was becoming known as a weirdo. After each rejection Samuel would sink into a depression, rancid with disappointment.

One day Anita Goodman from the Anita Goodman Gallery came to Louisa's studio for a visit. Louisa had worked hard presenting her paintings, and had even touched up the walls with white paint to cover the smears of color. She wanted Anita to see a show, not a studio. Anita was six-foot-two with gray streaks in her dark hair and she wore platform shoes, which made her enormous. Louisa came up to her nipples. This was a big deal, it was a good gallery. The seven paintings hanging on the walls looked very strong, very idiosyncratic.

Anita looked at each image for a long time and said, "I'd like to give you a show. You're going to need five more paintings." Louisa's elation instantly evaporated into anxiety. The slot was in September. It was May. There was still time for Samuel.

Before Anita left, Louisa said, casually, "Are you looking for new artists?"

"I'm always looking," said Anita, applying bronze lipstick to her generous mouth.

"Because I know a guy—he's really brilliant."

"What's his name?"

"Samuel Shapiro."

Anita smirked. "I know Shapiro. He's good. But—his stuff's not for me."

Louisa told Samuel about her show two days later while they were walking down the street. He just turned around and disappeared into the crowd. She didn't see him for a week.

. . .

Louisa had a dream in which a white bull was led by two men into an underground grotto. The bull was huge. Its muscles twitched beneath its skin. It was frightened. Louisa felt sorry for the bull and tried to pull the men away from it. The beast was bellowing piteously, bucking and pawing the ground. Its penis was bound tightly to its body with a thick rope wrapped around its midsection. All the friction made it come. Sperm sprayed around the grotto and Louisa tasted it. It was cold cream. One of the men held the animal's head back, gripping it by a horn, and removed a butcher knife from his pants pocket. Louisa screamed as the man slashed the animal's throat. Blood gushed from the wound. The bull fell to its knees, trying to raise itself. Slowly the life spurted and sputtered out of it. The bull lay dead on the ground.

She had the dream again, and then again. She began to paint the dream.

. . .

She made five large paintings. Each image was a stage in the sacrifice of the bull—dragging him into the grotto, the struggle, the ejaculation, the sacrifice, the death. She found herself holding her breath a lot while she was painting. When Samuel came to her studio to see the work for the first time, Louisa was choked with anticipation. He walked in and looked at the paintings one by one, silent. Then he sat down. He looked like he was going to faint.

"How could you?" he asked.

"How could I what?"

"How could you steal from me?"

"What are you talking about?"

"The bull."

"The bull comes from my dreams. I've been having dreams about that bull."

"It's a Mithraic sacrifice. I told you about them. They took a bull to a grotto and slit his throat. I painted them. You stole them from my paintings." The bull. The bull in Samuel's paintings. He had been slaughtered, along with several other animals, in the background of a couple of Samuel's canvases. Also Iphigenia.

"I wasn't thinking about your bull."

"How can you say that?"

Louisa looked at her bull, at his massive flanks, his tiny head, his sharp horns. But she hadn't been stealing. They were her dreams.

"Samuel, you're wrong."

"Just because you had a few dreams about a bull means you can steal my ideas? My work is about sacrifice. I have nothing Louisa, nothing but my ideas, my work, and you're stealing them from me."

"I—I'm sorry."

"Why didn't you—"

"I didn't mean—I wasn't—"

"You didn't warn me. Nothing."

" I wasn't thinking about your bull!"

"How can you—"

"I wasn't! If I did think about it I thought how amazing it was that our work overlapped in such deep ways, it made me feel close to you."

Samuel snorted. "You're completely corrupt," he said. Then he walked out the door, his face a bloodless mask.

Louisa stood in her studio and looked at her paintings. They were hers. She had made them, they had sprung from her head. He called her at two that morning, called every hour until seven. He wanted her to destroy the paintings. She cried on the phone, she pleaded with him, she threw down the phone. He was wearing away her resistance. She was becoming more and more uncertain of herself. It was true she had thought many times of how Samuel would solve certain problems, and his bull had flashed in her mind occasionally, though she had never felt guilty or a sense of doing wrong. And the style of the paintings—the form was completely different. Yet they were a cycle, and Samuel worked in cycles. And they were about sacrifice. His sense of righteousness burned into her brain through the telephone. He was like an avenging angel. Suddenly Louisa felt herself becoming everyone that had slighted him, that had ripped him off. She was the art world. She was evil.

Louisa felt as if she'd killed someone in her sleep.

. . .

At eight o'clock in the morning Louisa took out her pen-knife and plunged it into the throat of her first bull, right where the blood came out. She pulled the knife down through the canvas, making a slash across the surface of the painting. Then she stuck the knife into her wrist.

She called Sam from the emergency waiting room. She'd missed the big veins but she was bleeding quite a bit anyway. Sam came right away and sat with her in the sad choppy sea of people needing attention. Louisa's face was distorted from crying, her hair a snarled mass cascading over her shoulder.

"He says he owns the image of a bull?" Sam said. "What about the image of Christ—is that in any of his paintings? 'Cause if it is, he's got a lot of calls to make. Fuck. Louisa!"

"You don't understand," she said. "I think subconsciously or maybe even semiconsciously I adopted his—his sensibil-ity, or something."

"It's not like you killed a chicken and painted the judg-ment of Paris with its blood. That would be fishy. Your paint-ings are in a completely different style. Plus you always had

that mythic stuff in common. You know, I have to say something. I don't like Samuel's work."

"I know you don't."

"No—but you know why? It's tacky. It's heavy-handed.
It's gimmicky. It's obvious. It's full of Slavonic overload. It
has no lightness, and no truth." Louisa couldn't help smiling. The rag that was wrapped around her wrist was soaked
with blood, she was tenth in line in the Saint Vincent's emergency room, but Sam was here, so everything was all right.
She looked over at him. Brother.

"He's crazy, Louisa. How is it that everyone can see that
but you?"

. . .

Louisa's show was well reviewed by Alan Epstein of *The
New York Times,* who adored the paintings of middle-aged
mermaids. She sold seven pieces. She had a real chance at a
career now. The opening party was packed. Even Bruno
showed up with his gang—most of them rising stars in the art
world by now. Louisa smiled and talked but guilt was eating
into her happiness like acid. She knew why she had plunged
the knife into her wrist. She had done it so she wouldn't have
to destroy the rest of her paintings. The impulse had risen out
of the darkness of her ambition like Poseidon from the sea,

snatching her from the waves. There was something calculated about it. She suspected herself.

The morning after the opening, Samuel Shapiro called her. There had been a snowstorm the night before and the city was weirdly hushed as Louisa walked through the soft white streets to meet him, her boots squeaking in the new snow. A man passed her on skis.

Samuel was waiting for her in a corner of the dim café. He stood up when she reached the table, helped her with her coat. She ordered a hot chocolate. He had been crying.

"I was wrong," he said.

"About what?"

"I shouldn't have asked you to destroy the paintings. I'm sorry. I'm so sorry." A tear rolled down his cheek. "I just— that stuff doesn't matter," he said, looking at the table.

"You mean you still think I stole your stuff but you forgive me."

"I mean I love you."

She had never seen him weep before. It made her cry. His eyes lit up for a moment.

"Why are you crying?" he asked.

"Because it's all so fucking sad."

"Let's just—start really easy," he said. "Let's just see what happens. I think I can change, Louisa." She started to believe him. He put his hand over hers; her flesh hurt where he touched her.

"I have to get out of here," she said. Then she ran out of the café, ran all the way to Canal Street, and pulled the phone out of the wall.

She sat in silence the rest of the day watching the light change in her studio. When night fell she slept fitfully. She woke up at four A.M with ugly fragments of dreams in her head: a man hiding behind a door; children screaming. A month passed. She couldn't paint. She didn't see anyone. Her thirtieth birthday came and went. One day she wandered to the bus station and bought a ticket to go upstate. She didn't even warn her parents. She would call them from the bus stop.

As she stared down at Harlem from the bus, Louisa thought about the shape her life was taking. She felt as if she were acting out a text over which she had no control. She knew she would survive this. There would be new work, another relationship to fuck up. She would just keep leaving until no one wanted her anymore. She would never make a home, never settle down. She was restless. She was thrashing around in her sleep waiting for a prince, but there was no prince only postcards of princes. The only real one was Sam. The rest were carbon copies. And yet even Sam bore the mark of Seth's shadow. In the end the original was a ghost, the baby she had shared Penny's womb with.

. . .

In the attic of her parents' house, Louisa stood up. The ceiling was so low that she brushed it with the top of her head. It was dinnertime. She felt spent and strangely peaceful. She sat down at the table with her parents. Derk put the platter of meat before her. She put a hamburger into a bun and took a bite. The juice of the meat spread out across her tongue. It tasted salty and delicious. There was a spare patty on the platter, charred and oozing. Automatically Louisa's eyes went to the empty space beside her, Seth's place. He was there. He was always there. Penny was talking about buying delphiniums. She was halfway through her third glass of Chianti and her voice sounded like it was coated in Vaseline. Louisa felt the familiar fist of rage closing around her gut. She looked at Derk. He was chewing, staring out into the distance, as remote as a beast in a field. Then her eyes shifted back to Penny. Her mother was looking at her with such love that Louisa could hardly bear to see it; it was like looking into the sun. She wanted to look away but she didn't. This one time she didn't look away. The sun dipped below the tree line and the last light of dusk faded from Penny's face. Louisa could barely make out her features. But she was still there.

Julianne

Julianne Stein was standing naked in front of her large floor-length bathroom mirror. In the soft light coming through the open window she looked glorious, for forty-one. Rosy nipples on pear-shaped breasts, a strong stomach, hard, rounded thighs. She turned around and looked back at herself. The behind was a bit of a problem in that it didn't match the rest of her. It was large and round and fat. It was like a separate being. Most of the time Julianne liked it. Today it looked a little droopy. She stepped up to the mirror, turned on the overhead light, and scanned her body inch by inch.

From this close it was another story. Slowly, almost imperceptibly, Julianne was withering, like a peach left too long in the fridge. The flesh had begun to recede from the skin. The edges of the aureoles were beginning to pucker, the breasts were flattening, the delicate skin at the hinges of her arms was crinkling like rice paper. Someday the meat will have shrunk to a tiny ball in the center of her being, leaving a shriveled hide to move through the world. The changes in her body made Julianne feel as though she were sliding away from herself. She wondered how she would feel once the woman in the mirror was nobody she knew. How did one learn to act old? Maybe she would cut her hair, start wearing golf skirts.

Julianne stepped into the marble shower and thought about dinner. She would have to poach the salmon by four. The pesto would have to come out of the freezer. George and Mags were bringing a cake. Bread, she thought as she dried herself off. And she would have to cut some flowers. Wrapped in her fluffy chenille robe, her hair swaddled in a thick terry-cloth towel, Julianne felt heavy and warm. She walked into the shadowy bedroom, which smelled of narcissus, and lay down on the soft bed. Every surface of the room was jammed with framed photographs—Julianne and Joe on their wedding day, Julianne looking impossibly young and rounded and happy, Joe like a great big coal miner on a Sunday; Joe holding tiny Daisy cupped in his hands, the day she was born; Julianne and Daisy on a fishing trip; Joe's dour parents outside the coal mine where his father had worked, the only Jewish coal miner in Meeks, Pennsylvania; Julianne's plump, pampered mother with her brother Michael in her lap. "Everyone, everyone's here," she thought as she drifted off to sleep.

. . .

Julianne dreamed she was staying in a hotel on the seaside. She was alone. Her mouth felt full and warm. She got up, went to the mirror, and opened her lips. Her teeth were gone. All but one broken shard, loose in bloody gums awash in spit.

. . .

She woke sick with panic, her tongue sliding along the back of her strong teeth. In a haze of fear she pulled on pants and a sweater. She felt cold. She heard running. It was her daughter, Daisy. Daisy was always running or inert. She charged into her mother's room and wrapped her arms around a thigh, clinging to her like a limpet.

"Mama, I'm bored," she said.

"Why not play with the puppy?" asked Julianne.

"Um, he's sleeping."

"What about a nap?"

"I'm not sleepy. I'm bored."

"You ding-a-ling. Let's go see Pop," said Julianne. That's what she wanted, to see Joe.

"Is that okay?"

"It's almost four. I say it's okay." The child looked doubtful. She held her father's working habits as a sacred rule but would interrupt her mother to show her a broken nail. They walked down the hill to Joe's studio, a small one-room wooden structure with a chimney and three windows on one side, none on the other. Patches of sunlight on the forest floor glowed like luminescent leaves. Julianne watched the child's black hair glint blue in the light as she ran, excited to be seeing her father. Julianne felt that Daisy needed her, but she wasn't sure she loved her. Her little daughter came to her with earaches, stomach cramps, knotted hair, and bad dreams, but when all was well she turned firmly to Joe, her big old Daddy. She adored him. Joe looked preoccupied when Julianne knocked on the studio door.

"Come on in, ladies. Everything all right?"

"We missed you," said Julianne. Daisy climbed into Joe's lap.

Joe looked at his watch. "I'll be up in fifteen minutes," he said, smiling haplessly, his anger at being interrupted diluted by the sweetness of the call.

"*Andromeda* magazine is going to publish 'Winter Dream,'" Julianne said.

"That's fabulous, sweetie!" said Joe. "That's great."

"It's just a women's poetry journal. You know, advertisements for past-life therapy, lesbian talk lines."

"I think I've heard of it." He had no idea what she was talking about. "When did you hear?"

"This morning. Peter called."

"Why didn't you tell me?"

Julianne could tell he wanted to get back to work. She shrugged, looking at the floor.

"I don't—usually like the poems in that magazine."

"But you like your poem."

"I don't know anymore."

Julianne's poems were overripe, swollen with images of pistils and stamens and pregnant cows. She was like a traveler who overpacks time and again, only to regret it when she has to lug it all through customs. Her moist verbiage had earned her spots in women's poetry journals and she'd published one book, thanks largely to Joe's influence. Her work was too fecund for the serious literary magazines. She tried and tried to write a bony, rough, true poem. But they all came out as fleshy and ungovernable as her behind.

"What's the matter, Julianne?" Joe asked, swiveling his seat away from his typewriter with a sigh as Daisy snuggled into his chest.

"I had a bad dream."

"Tell me." Joe always wanted to hear about Julianne's dreams. She had come to suspect his curiosity; more than one of her unconscious images had ended up in his poems. She shook her head, looking at Daisy, who was dreamily twirling her hair around her finger.

"Go out and play, Mouse," he said. Daisy bolted out the door. Julianne started to cry.

"I dreamed all my teeth had fallen out," she said. "It was so horrible."

"Teeth dreams," said Joe. "Yuch."

"Will you love me when I have no teeth?" she asked.

"I would, honey, but I'm pretty sure you'll have to fit your dentures without me."

"Ssh," she said, climbing into his lap. She hated it when he talked about dying. He was sixty-nine. When they met he was fifty-three. She was twenty-five, a graduate student in the English department where he taught a seminar on Keats. The Great Man had just gotten divorced from his third wife, a manic-depressive hemophiliac. He'd been through it all— alcoholism, sobriety; cancer, surviving cancer; being hailed as a genius, being forgotten, being unearthed and praised again. His face was a mass of deep, crazy lines, as if someone had pried off his skin, crumpled it up like a piece of paper, and stuck it on again. It was hard to imagine anyone having so many wrinkles. When he met Julianne, he wanted a quiet life, he wanted slippers, and he wanted a child. Julianne wanted none of those things, not yet. But her body and her mind were being pulled toward Joe by a force she took to be destiny. At twenty-five Julianne was a vision. When they first spoke Joe said, "You look like a glass of milk." She was ful-some and shiny, with white teeth, full breasts, and thick hair—life on a plate. He said making love to her was like falling into a vat of gardenias and landing on a lovely fat sleepy sow. She took it as a compliment. They were married in a field. His only request was that she never again use the word "succulent" in a poem.

Joe shifted Julianne's weight on his knee and sighed. Julianne stood up.

"I have to poach the salmon," she said.

He patted her thigh and swiveled back to look at the page he was typing. Julianne looked at it too. He had written: "Quick black eyes in a blackened face / your scrubbed hands pale as doves / lie spent and broken on the table." Tears of envy came to her eyes. She knew the poem would be bony, it would be rough, it would be true.

She wrapped a whole salmon in cheesecloth and lay its soft body gently into a shallow earthenware pot. She kneaded bread dough, putting her whole weight into the heels of her hands, sweat on the back of her neck, and out of the corner of her eye she glimpsed her other life, the life she would have had without Joe. The other Julianne was sitting in front of a typewriter by a window in her old apartment in New York, gazing out into the dusk, a cigarette between her fingers. No, no cigarette. Coffee. The typewriter had a sheet of paper arching out of it, and there were two stanzas, two sharp, clean, perfect stanzas, hammered into the meat of the page. Julianne stopped kneading and stood perfectly still for a moment. Her other self had disappeared and she was, for a moment, wholly present in her own life. She would never write a great poem. She had married a great man instead. She was a kneader of bread dough, a poacher of salmon. She had trapped herself. She would never be any good because she didn't have time.

. . .

The evening was unfolding smoothly. The first course was almost finished and Joe was telling one of his favorite stories. It was a tale Julianne usually thought hilarious, about a sign painter from Florida named Al Kohalic who drank too much. But tonight Julianne let her mind drift away from her husband's voice as she watched her daughter. Daisy was on her father's lap, wearing a nightgown with rabbits on it. She had been woken up by a particularly loud burst of laughter downstairs and once she was in her father's lap, that was it for the evening. Julianne watched her daughter's earnest, pale little face. She never seemed to be listening to a thing anybody said but Julianne knew she was absorbing it all, hoarding it inside herself until one day she would explode with poetry. Daisy wasn't going to be pretty, and although Julianne pitied her for it she envied her, too. Julianne had been too beautiful and it had warped everything. Now that she felt her looks fading even her old poems seemed to be getting worse, as if the words in them had been buoyed by her beauty, lifted out of themselves and up, toward a greater destiny than they had deserved, the destiny of a beautiful woman. Now they seemed to be sinking as ineluctably as her tits. She looked at Joe, who was commanding the company as he came to the climax of his tale, animated and slightly flushed from the wine.

He married me like an old man marries his nurse, she thought. *He's always been slightly embarrassed by my poems. He's kind about it but he's given up on me as a writer. These people*—she looked around at the sampling of intellectuals gathered at the table, all weathered, myopic, wry, brilliant. *These people don't even see me. They see Joe's pretty wife who isn't quite so pretty anymore, the one who writes the ghastly poetry.*

She drained her glass and got up petulantly to whip the cream for the cake. She had had a few glasses of wine—she rarely drank—and her fingers felt rubbery as she pawed through the cluttered drawer looking for the eggbeater. As she started to whip the cream, she heard a horrible sound of an animal screaming. At first Julianne thought the dog had been hit by a car and somehow gotten into the kitchen. She wheeled around and saw her cleaning lady, whom she sometimes hired for the evening, standing three feet away from her, gripping the counter, yelping.

"Mrs. Doyle?" she said. "Mrs. Doyle!" Mrs. Doyle, a very tall, knock-kneed woman with frizzy red hair, seemed to be terrified. Her hands were clutching the kitchen counter as if some fierce wind were trying to rip her away from it; her eyes were wide and fixed. Julianne hugged her. She didn't know what else to do. By this time Joe was standing at the threshold, ready to take over. Julianne waved him away. She could feel the woman's muscles relaxing. Slowly Mrs. Doyle allowed herself to be guided over to a chair.

"Mrs. Doyle," Julianne whispered in the woman's ear. "Bryna. You're among friends, Bryna." The woman slumped down in her chair, exhausted from her fit, and looked at Julianne intently through her frightened blue eyes. Her skin was very pale and soft. She was wearing orange lipstick. Julianne stroked her hand. Mrs. Doyle had been with the Steins for seven years but Julianne knew very little about her life. She and her taciturn husband worked the small dairy farm down the road. She had two grown children. She was always cheerful. Suddenly Mrs. Doyle burst into a convulsion of tears, clutching Julianne's hand with such strength that it hurt her. Julianne winced, but she didn't pull her hand away.

"I'm so sorry," said Mrs. Doyle.

"You ought to get home," said Julianne.

Julianne drove Mrs. Doyle home in the old Jaguar. They were silent on the brief journey out the driveway, up the hill, over the crest, and down into the shallow valley where the

Doyles' little farmhouse sat across the street from their
quaintly decomposing barn. When they reached the house,
Mrs. Doyle made no move to get out of the car. She just sat
staring straight ahead. Julianne was beginning to wonder if
she should go get Mr. Doyle so he could pull his wife out of
the car. But that seemed like a betrayal. There was trust in
Mrs. Doyle's silence. A light went on upstairs.

"You have such a lovely barn," said Julianne. "I always
slow down to have a look at it when I go by." Her words
sounded idiotic to her. A long moment passed. Finally Mrs.
Doyle moved—she lurched forward and her hand went out
blindly to the door handle.

"If you ever need to talk to anyone," Julianne said softly,
"I . . . well, you can talk to me if you want."

"Thank you," said Mrs. Doyle. Then she opened the door
and walked stiffly into the house. Julianne watched as the
screen door slammed closed behind her cleaning woman, a
mystery to her now. Who was Bryna Doyle? Julianne looked
across the road, at the Doyles' little farm, the aged silo list-
ing slightly, lit up by the brilliant moon. Behind the barn a
gentle hill sloped up to the black tree line, where the forest
began. Julianne felt great tenderness as she looked at the
collapsing barn, the long brown grass dying around it. It
hadn't rained for a month. How long would the Doyles be
able to survive, she wondered. How long before there were

strangers in this little house, pulling off the roof to make a skylight, turning the barn into a recording studio or an antiques shop, or the hill bitten up by imitation colonial homes? Everything was changing, everything was going away, why couldn't things stay the way they were? How many more times would Julianne hear Joe's story about Al Kohalic? Tonight might have been the last time, and she hadn't even been listening. And Daisy—Daisy! Her warm soft hands seeking out Julianne's face to caress in the dark, like a baby again when she was half asleep—Daisy needed her still. How many more times would she run into Julianne's room and throw her arms around her thighs? Twenty? Sixty? A hundred? The fragile grace of her life at that moment filled Julianne with wonder and shame. She saw Mrs. Doyle silhouetted in the lit window for a moment, and then the light went out.

You ding-a-ling, Julianne thought.

She turned her car around and sped back home.

Bryna

As Bryna Doyle reached across the table to clear up the remains of her husband's breakfast she happened to glance out the window at the barn. Milton was standing there with a bucket in his hand, watching a horse eat. And the horse was watching Milton. Bryna took hold of his plate and looked over at the old lady sitting in her red plush armchair. Elbows on her bony knees, she was staring out the window in a posture of rigid attention. Her black eyes were screwed up against the harsh early light, her mouth slightly agape, as if the sight of her son standing motionless before a horse were the Barnum & Bailey circus.

Milt's mother had been hogging that red plush chair for twenty-seven years, ever since her husband died and she finally got the chance. Pop Doyle had presided in the chair every evening of his adult life, growling and snatching at the children when he was surly, throwing them up into the air when he was cheerful. He once killed the family dog with his bare hands, snapped its neck to stop its barking. It wasn't surprising that Milt grew up practically mute. He was the baby of the family, the only boy after a passel of girls, and the old lady decided to keep him for herself. She carried him around on her hip until he was two, and when the old man died she wedged herself into the red plush chair and set up house with her thirty-year-old son. For five years they lived as seamlessly as an old married couple. Then one day Milt had to go to Albany to get a root canal. Bryna was working as a secretary in the dentist's office, living with her aunt in the city, buying stockings and movie magazines, going to the pictures with her girlfriends, and daydreaming about a glamorous life with Paul Newman or some ad executive or maybe even Dr. Berg the dentist, who knew, when this rube shuffles into the office, mud on his boots, cheeks bright red the minute he laid eyes on her. She was nice to him; it was painful to look at him he was so shy. A week after his appointment he walked back through the doors and stepped up to Bryna's desk, his hands dangling by his sides. It was pouring out and his clothes were soaked. Bryna looked up efficiently.

"Hello, Mr. Doyle," she said. She could hear the air whistling through the hairs in his nose. "Did you forget something?" Milt leaned forward, placing his wet, thick, reddish fingers on Bryna's green-felt ink blotter, and looked at her with a deliberate, unwavering gaze. Bryna could tell he was steeling himself against the force of his diffidence. She felt her stomach freeze up for him. A droplet of water fell from his nose and spread dark on the blotter.

"You want to get a cup of coffee some time?" he said.

"All right," she heard herself say. "Just a cup of coffee. Yes."

They went to a sandwich shop and the waitress asked her if she wanted cheese on her ham sandwich. Bryna declined.

After about five minutes, Milt said, "You don't like cheese?"

"It's not that . . ." said Bryna.

"Me neither."

That was it for the date. There was something about Milt that made Bryna feel safe. He seemed to be something you could count on forever, like a boat on cinder blocks in somebody's backyard far inland where it would never touch the sea again. The wedding was small; Bryna's family was in Toronto. The old lady took against Bryna on impact. She derided her lumpy looks, her squeamishness, her glossy magazines. And she suspected her of harboring a secret, crafty intelligence beneath her bumbling exterior. This hunch was borne out when both Bryna's children were almost eerily good in school and proceeded to get into top colleges on full scholarships. Brains in a woman was like a hidden river, the old lady always said, it could pop out from under a rock and drown you anytime.

The soapy brush swept across the chipped blue plate in an elegant arc, leaving a film of tiny bubbles and dissolving the crust of egg. As Bryna bathed the dish serenely in the sink, wearing bright pink rubber gloves, a smug little smile crept onto her face and her eyebrows raised slightly; she was listening to something.

"Well," she said very softly, so softly that almost no sound came out. "I've never been one for hasty washing. I like to take my time with the dishes—to get myself ready for the rest of the day. . . . Hm? Oh, well, usually I take my walk, though sometimes I visit friends."

Bryna couldn't remember when she had started being interviewed. It was so long ago now that the process was as natural as breathing. A few times a day she would have a little chat with the interviewer—a journalist from *Redbook*, *Women's Wear Daily*, or *TV Guide*, as a rule, explaining just how she made tuna casserole, how she seasoned Mr. Doyle's oatmeal, how she chose her lipstick for the day.

Once the dishes were finished, she poured a cup of tea and took it to the old lady, who had been dozing. "See you later, Mother," she said.

"All right-y," said the old lady ironically, extending a veiny hand to take the tea.

Bryna walked across the narrow road, the keys to the truck jingling in her hand. She was a very tall woman, with large feet and hands. Her hair was reddish and fine and floated in a cloud around her head, even though she was always trying to tame it with curlers. Today she was wearing a baby-blue cotton short-sleeved blouse, a pair of brown polyester pants that were an inch and a half too short, white socks, and a pair of penny loafers. None of the Doyles' mirrors extended past the waistline, so Bryna tended to look eccentric from the thighs down. Milt was in the barn. She could hear the radio on in there. Bryna leaned on the wooden fence and called out—

"Milt?" No answer. "Milt!" She waited. It was hot in the sun. She could feel the eyes of the old lady on her, staring through the window. "MILT!" Milt didn't come out so she gave the fence a shove, irritated now. It gave way, dragging sluggishly along the long brown grass. She pushed it shut and walked over to the door of the barn. Tentatively she looked inside, craning her body over the door frame while keeping her feet safely outside it. Milt was mucking out the stallion's stall, scraping the pitchfork just behind the animal's massive gray thighs. The music was on pretty loud. "I really love your peaches. Want to shake your tree . . ." He didn't care what he listened to. "Milt!" He worked on, oblivious. She wouldn't go inside. Hadn't. Ever. Not the barn. It had started as a fear of being kicked and developed into fear of the barn.

"MILTON!" This time he heard her. Turned off the radio.

"I have to be at the Steins, I'm almost late."

Milt wiped his hands on his blue coveralls, locked the stall, and wordlessly took the keys from his wife's hand. They crossed the road and got into the truck.

It hadn't rained in six weeks and the grass was dry as cornflakes. The cows couldn't graze, all the feed had to be bought. The well was down forty feet. Neighbors had run out of water entirely. Bryna could feel Milt's worry in the pit of her stomach. They had already taken in horses to board. How long could they hold out? She looked over at her husband's big dry cracked hands on the steering wheel. His eyes were blue, pale blue like jeans washed too many times. He had blond lashes. Bryna looked out the window. The sky was cloudless. Another cruel day. They turned into the Steins' driveway. Milt stopped at the entrance. He didn't want to have to have a conversation and those people were always trying to draw him out. Local color.

"I'll see you at lunch," Bryna said.

"See you," he said.

Bryna walked up the drive. As she rounded the fine magnolia tree that, along with several raggedy hedges, obscured the front of the house, she came upon Joe Stein, the famous poet and novelist, reciting something loudly into a bush just outside the door, his back to her.

"Doctor, doctor," he said in a growling voice, "take the infant back."

Bryna kept walking, head down, wondering if she should say hello as she passed or just walk into the house as if Mr. Stein wasn't there, when she heard the steady, full sound of piss hitting the ground. She froze, holding her breath. She couldn't just pass by him while he was relieving himself. And she couldn't retreat, she might step on a twig. He was a foot away, she could have blown on his neck. All she could do was hope that he wouldn't turn around. It was taking forever. "Put me in the ward with all the thin grim fellows—" Mr. Stein was a big, hunched man with skin like a rhino and almost entirely bald, yet he had been married four times to beautiful women. What could she possibly say if he turned around? It would look as if she'd been spying on him. She felt beads of sweat rise on her upper lip. "Who have suffered and pulled through." Finally the stream trickled to a halt. "Don't make me antiseptic, white, and fat." Mr. Stein zipped up his fly, took a couple of steps toward the house, then suddenly wheeled around and stepped right into Bryna, sucking in his breath.

"Mrs. Doyle!" She had scared him.

"Oh hi Mr. Stein, I was just walking up to the house," Bryna said in her full, slightly muffled voice that seemed to come from somewhere in the back of her throat.

"Lucky you didn't come up a minute ago, I was, ah, having a pee in the hedge—we all are—saving water, you know," said Mr. Stein, his face crinkling into a lopsided smile. Bryna stepped to one side. She wanted to get into the house.

"Does Milt think it's going to rain soon?" Mr. Stein asked.

"Yes, yes he does," said Bryna.

"Well let's hope he's right!" said Mr. Stein, disappearing behind a hedge. He was going to his studio, Bryna knew, a grimy little shack in the woods. Thank God he never wanted her to clean it. She imagined there were spiders in there. Mr. Stein always made her nervous.

In the kitchen, Bryna started washing the few dirty dishes little Daisy had left in the sink. (Mrs. Stein always did the dishes before Bryna got there so that she could concentrate on the bigger cleaning issues.) There was as always a little apple tart waiting for her on the counter, under a piece of paper towel, along with a peach-colored envelope containing the week's wages. Just then Daisy, the Steins' eight-year-old daughter, ran in barefoot.

"Hi Mrs. Doyle," she mumbled, opening the refrigerator and looking into it for a really long time, as if whatever she felt like eating would materialize if she waited long enough. Eventually she swung the door shut and ran out of the room.

Bryna was vacuuming the stairs when Mrs. Stein came wafting out of her bedroom wearing a beautiful long red Chinese dressing gown.

"Hello, Mrs. Doyle," she said. "How are you?" Bryna felt a lump rise in her throat, she didn't know why. She looked down at the vacuum cleaner.

"Fine," she said.

"Is it still all right for you to come back this evening for the party?"

"Yes, it's all right," said Bryna.

Mrs. Stein went downstairs, leaving Bryna in a cloud of tea-rose perfume. Bryna would never have guessed how old Mrs. Stein was if she hadn't seen her driver's license. She was forty-one—almost the same age as Bryna! Yet she seemed like a girl. She had wavy, light-brown hair that framed her face and clear hazel eyes. She always seemed to be off swimming. And she had some work that she did shut away in her little office off the master bedroom. Bryna loved emptying Mrs. Stein's personal trash. There were always mysterious shreds of letters in it, with words like "gush" and "cusp" scrawled across them in scented lavender ink. Bryna never tried to put the fragments together—she would have considered it an intrusion. But she did enjoy reading the scraps; they intimated a secret, delicious life. When Bryna read romantic novels, she usually imagined the heroine as Mrs. Stein.

"Stein residence, Mrs. Doyle speaking."

Bryna always answered the Stein phone like that; it seemed so much better than "hello," which might not have been appropriate since she didn't live there, and "Stein residence" was so impersonal.

"Is Julianne Cohen there please?" A man with an accent. Mrs. Doyle was silent for a moment.

"Mrs. Stein is unavailable." She had just seen her employer go off toward the pool with a towel over her arm.

"Could you please tell her that Peter Stonstrom is calling? It's quite important."

"All right," said Bryna coolly. "Please hold on." She marched off down the hill to the pool. Mrs. Stein was doing the backstroke naked. Her breasts rose and fell through ripples of water as her arms churned the water in regular, swift stokes. "Mrs. Stein?" said Bryna, trying to stay as far away as possible. Mrs. Stein didn't hear her. "Mrs. Stein?" Nothing. "Mrs. Stein! Mrs. Stein! Mrs. Stein!" Bryna ran along the edge of the pool waving her arms. She looked like an enormous, fluffy bird trying to take off. Mrs. Stein saw her and stopped.

"What's happened?" she said.

"A man on the phone. Mr. Stoneman. He says it's urgent."

Mrs. Stein swam, smiling, to the edge of the pool and pulled herself out. Her body was rounded and firm and shiny, like a polished stone sculpture. Bryna handed her the yellow towel from the bench, looking at the flagstone. Mrs. Stein didn't even seem to notice she was naked.

"Thank you so much, Mrs. Doyle," she said, wrapping the towel around herself loosely and trotting up toward the house. Bryna watched. It was hard to believe anybody could be that beautiful.

When Byrna got to the end of the Steins' driveway, Milt had been waiting for fifteen minutes. As she walked through the kitchen door, the old lady stared at her as if she'd set fire to the carpet. It was quarter to one. Lunch was at twelve-thirty. Bryna didn't say anything, she just got out the ham and bread, made a sandwich for the old lady, who fell on it ravenously in her chair, and started eating her own sandwich. The three of them chewed in silence for a while.

"What kind of ham is this?" asked Milt.

"Smoked."

"It's good."

After a few more swallows he was off to the barn. The old lady drank down the dregs of her apple juice and, as was her custom, got up to go to the john. As she passed, Bryna smelled the musk that always clung to the old lady's person even though she seemed to wash regularly. Her towel was wet anyway. Something about the way the old lady shuffled up the stairs filled Bryna with animosity. Her eyes fell on the red plush chair. She had never sat in that chair. Her children hadn't sat in it, Milt hadn't sat in it. It looked insolent, taking up the best spot in the kitchen, the one place where the sun shone really warm and bright. It looked judgmental, as if obliged to disapprove of Bryna while the old lady was taking a crap. Somebody had to.

At five-thirty, Bryna was in her cramped bedroom getting clothes out for working at the Steins' party. She always wore black and white to serve at their evenings. Mrs. Stein never requested it but Bryna felt it was the right thing to do. She was tempted to wear the white silk blouse her daughter, Sheila, had brought her back from Paris, where she was studying. But then it might get stained. She lifted the blouse out of the drawer gently and let the silk fall through her fingers. It didn't feel like cloth at all. It felt like cold liquid, or the way a cloud must feel if you wave your hand through it. She remembered looking down through the blue at the layer of clouds from the airplane—they looked solid, fluffy and silken. Bryna had been in an airplane twice, the flight to Paris to visit Sheila and the flight home. She had gotten everything packed two weeks ahead of time. She and Milt even made a dry run to the airport just to be sure they knew the way. But when they got to Paris, Milt was silent for three days. He just sat there, staring at his croissant and coffee or out the window of his room. Finally, on the fourth day, he said, "I want to go home." They had planned to stay two weeks.

Sheila was as tall as Bryna but her bones were delicate as a bird's. She had quick green eyes and long fingers, like her brother. Nathaniel was dark and serious, a reporter for the *Boston Globe*. When the Doyle kids came home to visit, it was as if they were from outer space. Bryna would just stand there in the tiny kitchen smiling at them and they at her, all of them marveling at the light years of distance between this moment of awkward goodwill and the days, not so long gone, when they were a family: the kids had chores, they were punished, they were praised. Nathaniel had looked up to his father and Sheila looked up to her mother. Then one day they went away and when they came back they were aliens in silk and tweed.

Bryna slipped on the blouse. It felt cool against her skin.

At nine o'clock Bryna was at the Steins' kitchen counter, sponging up a smear of guacamole, watching the company through the door that led into the dining room. The guests looked as if they were floating in candlelight. Mr. Stein, little Daisy on his lap, was telling a story in his deep rough voice and everyone was listening, rapt. He went silent and they all exploded in laughter. Bryna cocked her head dreamily to one side.

"Well," she whispered. "Whenever I have a party—I know this sounds bananas—first I make sure everyone is having a good time. Then I sneak into the kitchen and clean up a little. Even a few seconds of washing up—a dish here, a countertop there—makes a difference, and I hate to leave the maid with a great big mess."

Mrs. Stein stood up suddenly and rushed into the kitchen murmuring, "Whipped cream . . ." Bryna watched as Mrs. Stein fumbled in the utility drawer and got out the electric whisk. She was wearing a long red dress with little black beads embroidered into it. Her brown hair with its strands of gold was wound into a bun at the base of her long neck. As the metal blades churned the thick cream, little flecks of white splashed onto her smooth forehead. Mrs. Stein was perfect. Bryna felt a surge of yearning, wonder, and despair. She would always be Bryna. Forever Bryna Doyle.

Suddenly a cold wave passed through Bryna's belly and the walls went dark. The sounds in the next room were gone. All she could hear was a sort of whining in her head, like an insect. Sweat coated her palms and glided down her sides; her legs were locked in place like iron rods. All she could see was the white of the cream, glowing in the eclipsed room. The sound in her head was coming in bursts now—it sounded like the shrieks of a wounded animal. Bryna managed to take a step back. She thought if she could sit down she might be all right. *Sit down,* she thought. She glimpsed Mr. Stein's face through the door. He was looking at her, his face filled with bafflement, fear, and pity. Daisy had her head buried in his chest. Then Bryna realized that she was making the horrible sound herself. Mrs. Stein was next to her now. She had her arms around her. She was speaking but no sound was coming out of her mouth. Bryna went quiet, walked stiffly to the kitchen table, and sat down. She could hear again. Her breath was broken as if she had been sobbing. Mrs. Stein was pulling up a seat beside her. She was stroking her hand. Bryna felt laid bare, purged, and weirdly happy. She was with Mrs. Stein. She wanted to be with Mrs. Stein.

"What is it, Bryna?" asked Mrs. Stein. She had never called Bryna by her first name before. Bryna burst into tears. It felt as violent and embarrassing as vomiting in the street.

"I'm so sorry," she said.

"You ought to get home."

"I'll call Milt," said Bryna.

"No. I'll drive you," said Mrs. Stein.

When they got to the mouth of the Doyles' short driveway the two women sat together in silence for a long time. The Steins' car smelled of leather and cigarettes and rose perfume. Mrs. Stein said something very gently, but Bryna didn't really hear the words. The crickets outside were screaming, a wall of sound. Bryna wanted this moment never to end.

"Get out, Bryna," she said to herself. "You have to get out. Mrs. Stein has guests." It took a long time for her muscles to

obey her mind and when they did she moved clumsily, like a
sleepwalker. She wanted to say something; she was filled with
the urge to speak.

"Thank you, Mrs. Stein," she said.

Milt was waiting inside the kitchen door.

"What happened?" he asked.

"I didn't feel well."

"Want some tea?"

"You go on up to bed, you must be tired," she said.

"You too."

"I'm coming up in a second."

"All right."

Bryna watched as Milt lumbered up the stairs. He looked
back at her once as he opened the bathroom door at the top
of the staircase. Then he shut it. The white silk blouse was
soaked with cooling sweat. Bryna drew her jacket around her
and stared at the red plush chair. The light beside it was on;
it seemed spotlit, like the chair in a play she'd seen her daughter in. Bryna stared and stared without blinking until the chair
began to move very slightly. An hour passed. It was, after all,
only a chair, she thought. Bryna tried to get up but she
couldn't move. She tried again. Nothing. The velour was worn
thin where the old lady sat. Bryna was so tired that her eyes
felt dried out. With a lurch she heaved herself up, took three
steps, and let herself drop into the old lady's chair.

It was so comfortable. Perfect. The kitchen looked cozy from here, not cramped like it did from other angles. The blue and white flowered wallpaper seemed fresher, the buttery yellow paint on the cabinets looked like just the right choice. It seemed like a whole other house.

"Well . . ." Bryna said softly, crossing her legs and pursing her lips slightly. "This was a genuine country farmhouse so I went with a down-home feel. The details are very important in a project like this. Hm?" She strained forward now, as if to hear a question the interviewer was putting to her. "Oh. No. No, I don't think so," she said, pausing again. Now she sat back and chuckled. "Well, thank you. Thank you. We like it, anyway." Just then she heard footsteps shuffling along the hall upstairs. It was the old lady. Bryna's muscles tensed as if to get up but she stayed still. She heard the bathroom door creak open, and pause there. Bryna knew the old lady had seen her from the top of the stairs. She was watching Bryna. Bryna's heart was ramming itself against her chest. Finally the door shut. Bryna got up. Her feet were cold. She wanted to go to bed. The old lady was taking forever in the bathroom. Just to spite her, Bryna thought. Her bones ached. Finally, after fifteen minutes, she heard the old lady walk slowly down the hall and into her room.

When Bryna opened the door to the bathroom it took her a few seconds to realize what had happened. At first she thought the toilet had exploded. The walls were smeared in excrement. There was a great dollop of it in the sink. The beige shag rug was matted down with a shiny black oval, like an open sore on a dog. And the old lady had left a perfect little brown handprint in the center of the toilet seat, like a signature.

Bryna just stood there thinking about cleaning products. Mr. Clean, Ajax, Tub and Tile, Janitor in a Drum. She'd have to take up the rug, rip it right off the tacks. It was all right, she had another piece in the garage. When Milt walked in it was one in the morning and she was on her hands and knees. The walls and sink were nearly clean but the stench was horrible.

"She saw me sitting in her chair," she said.

"When?" he said.

"Tonight."

"What did you do that for?" Milt asked.

"I felt like it. I thought I was allowed to sit in any chair in my own house at eleven o'clock at night. I didn't see a line to get in it," she said.

"Oh boy," he said.

He helped her take up the rug and then took it outside in a trash bag. The floorboards were oak. Bryna hadn't ever known that. At about three A.M they had sweet tea and cookies in the kitchen. Then Bryna took a hot bath. She felt full and blank. Milt was waiting for her in bed. Once the light was out he reached for her in the dark and kissed her. She was surprised, but it felt nice. His lips were rough and cool; his tongue was soft and warm. Bryna closed her eyes and imagined that Milt had taken her to have a picnic in a secluded spot in the woods. He kept stroking her hands, her breasts, her hair . . . she had just started to unpack the sandwiches when she felt Milt's hand pass over her shut eyelids.

"Bryna," he said.

She opened her eyes and looked up at him. She could feel his breath on her face. He lay still above her, his hand stroking her cheek. He was warm. She felt so naked. Afterward she held Milt's rough hand and looked outside. The bright full moon filled the window frame. It seemed close enough to touch.

The next morning they slept till nine. Bryna was lured out of her dreams by the sound of rain hammering crazily against the window.

They came downstairs laughing. The old lady was sitting in her chair, glaring at them. She seemed smaller, as if she had shrunk in the night. Bryna looked into the old lady's black eyes and realized she was mad, stark raving mad.

"How are you feeling, Mother?" Milt asked.

"Fine, dear," she said.

"Maybe you should see a doctor."

"Why?"

Bryna brought the old lady an English muffin. Outside, the trees were bending in the wind.

Nancy

I am waiting. I hear him coming. I am waiting. I am waiting.

The child watches, quiet as a cat, as the stocky man shuffles across the Chinese carpet and sits down heavily in an armchair, opening the newspaper onto his knees. The girl likes to see how long she can be in a room without her father noticing her. She has driven her record up to one hour, seventeen minutes, and thirty-four seconds. Nancy is always competing with herself.

Last summer at the club pool in Southampton she increased the length of time she could hold her breath underwater minute by minute until one day she was submerged so long the lifeguard came diving in after her. She went limp as she felt him grab her and clench her to his side, dragging her up to the light. As they broke the surface of the water she twisted around and laughed in his face. The lifeguard's eyes widened. His arms chopped at the water as he backed away from her, the veins puffing out in his muscular neck like fat blue worms. Somebody snickered from the side of the pool.

"Little bitch," the lifeguard muttered. He turned and swam to the edge of the pool with a couple of powerful strokes, then pulled himself out of the water and clambered up the rungs of his high chair like a big monkey. Nancy watched as he settled back into the canvas seat, breathing hard. He spread his legs and put on a blank, insolent look that reminded her of a father gorilla she had seen at the zoo. The ape had sat apart from his family slowly chewing a banana, his hooded eyes regarding his children remotely as they hopped about in the sunshine.

But Nancy could tell that the lifeguard was embarrassed. She saw the hurt in his eyes. It made her feel thrilled and culpable. Each day for the rest of the summer she brought him fruit and candy, laying her offerings down gently at the base of his tall chair.

The afternoon darkness has bitten into the room, eating out the light until there is only a sliver of it on the floor. Nancy's father is staring down at the newspaper, his eyes fixed. A chrome lamp peers blindly over his shoulder, the bulb cold and dull as lead.

Music filters down through speakers set flush in the walls and covered with rough white linen.

The girl from Ipanema goes walking,
and as she passes each one she passes goes,
'Ah' . . .

The music swirls like water around the furniture, around the immobile forms of Nancy and her father.

The apartment is still as a stone garden. Nancy's mother is out, the cook is food shopping, the maid has gone home, and the weekend nanny is late.

Nancy has to pee. Her eyes dart from her father's face to the silver-plated clock her mother brought home from New Year's on the Concorde: 4:47. Just six more minutes of not being noticed and she will break her record. Her bladder is beginning to hurt—4:48 . . . 4:49 . . . 4:50. She tries counting the nails in the floorboard, twisting the string of her sweatshirt, pinching her leg. She glances at the bathroom door. Ten steps. She's going to have to risk it. She stands up, barely breathing, her eyes on her father, raises her foot, and sets it down without looking. A colored pencil shoots out from under her heel, clattering against the kickboard. Her father turns, startled.

"Why are you always sneaking around?" he says in his flat western drawl.

"I have to go to the bathroom," says Nancy, running into the toilet and locking the door. When she comes out her father is looking at her, frowning.

"Don't become a sneak," he says. "Commere." Nancy runs over to him, putting her little hands, still brown from Thanksgiving break in Saint Lucia, on his knees. "There are two kinds of people in this world," he says. "Lions and mice. You're not a mouse. Don't act like one." Then he sweeps the heavy blond hair back from her face with trembling fingers and asks, "What about your homework?"

"I did it," she lies.

"Where's Sarah?"

"She's not here yet."

"You can watch TV."

"None of my shows are on right now." Her father sighs and looks at her. Nancy has a perfect American face, just like her mother; the small nose, the flat, broad mouth. But her eyes are different.

Nancy's light blue eyes have the piercing gaze of a nineteenth-century settler child. She looks as though she ought to be on a horse, staring into the endless Wyoming sky. Instead she stares into Madison Avenue shop windows and wide-screen TVs. She is nine years old, yet she falls into womanly poses that make her father grin with embarrassment.

. . .

The weekend nanny is rising in the elevator. Sarah Green is a slight, ambitious young woman with a crooked back, hungry green eyes, and a quick smile. John Jo, the elevator man, glances at her. He doesn't care for her. Sarah is always staring at people in his elevator, sussing them. No warmth coming off her. John Jo stops the elevator with a jerk and yanks open the gate and door. Sarah steps off and smiles.

"Thanks," she says.

"Okay," says John Jo. The elevator creaks shut and Sarah turns to face the Dunnes' door. She doesn't touch the bell. She is gathering her thoughts.

Sarah is a year away from a master's degree in child psychology at Columbia. Nancy's mother hired her because she thought there might be something wrong with Nancy. It all started a year earlier, when Nancy locked little Gemma Stevenson into the utility closet. Nancy's mother heard the little girl screaming through the intercom. After a frantic search of the labyrinthine duplex, she found Gemma trembling and sobbing among the brooms. Nancy was on the bed in the maid's room, calmly leafing through one of her mother's magazines.

"How could you lock that little girl in the closet?" Nicole screamed. Nancy looked up at her mother serenely.

"I don't know what you're talking about," she said.

Nancy truly didn't understand what had happened. She was playing with Gemma in the kitchen, and suddenly she just needed to shove her into the closet. She turned the lock and Gemma started screaming, banging on the door. Nancy stood staring dumbly. Every second that passed made it less possible to let Gemma out. She turned and walked into the maid's room.

A stack of her mother's old *Bazaar* magazines were piled next to the bed. Nancy sat down on the pink bedspread and opened a glossy magazine, her heart hammering against the base of her throat. She could hear Gemma shrieking next door, desperate. On the page, a woman in a bikini was jumping on a trampoline, laughing. Nancy heard her mother running into the kitchen. There was a muffled noise and then Gemma's sobs, louder now, her mother soothing her. Nancy stared at the laughing woman, willing her mind dead.

There were other signs of trouble: taking money from her mother's purse, compulsive lying, sudden fits of hysteria. The last straw was when Nancy stole an American Express card at a birthday party. Nancy's mother got a call that evening from Lydia Peters, the birthday girl's mother. Giggling with embarrassment, Lydia said that Nancy had been alone in the master bedroom a long time. When she left the party the card was gone from the bedside table. Lydia hated to ask but . . . Nancy's mother found the card, cut it up, and called Lydia back, telling her coldly that Nancy was innocent.

Nicole found Sarah Green through a friend who had used her as a baby-sitter / mental-health monitor, and watched her daughter's progress from a distance, reluctant to send her to a real shrink. Nancy's mother had nothing against psychiatry. She was afraid it would get leaked to the press.

Town and Country Magazine, September 1999.

Nicole Dunne is no wallflower. The wife of Steven Dunne, world-class entrepreneur, self-made man, and avid horseman, she is known as much for her lively banter as for the imaginative twists she gives her glamorous parties both in Southampton and Manhattan.

"I never let the guest list go over two hundred," she says, flicking her blond hair behind her as we saunter through the French-style garden on her Southampton estate. "I want it to feel special, not like a damn fundraiser." Then she laughs, a throaty, worldly, girlish laugh, an infectious laugh that says as much about Nicole Dunne's appeal as anything she'll tell me for the rest of the afternoon. "I like theme parties—Moroccan with a French twist, 'La Dolce Vita,' even German once—I actually bought a dirndl!" she laughs, sipping iced tea served by her butler Jerry.

Whatever Nicole Dunne is doing, it's working. She has entertained Brooke Astor and Salman Rushdie under the same tent. Her parties are at the top of the list for all New York society.

Just as I am thinking that there must be a cloud on the golden horizon of Steven Dunne's beautiful and charismatic wife, Mr. Dunne himself walks through the door and kisses her on the lips. And I throw up my internal hands, thinking some people have all the luck. Steven Dunne is ruggedly handsome, with the thick, glossy hair of a Kennedy. He is quiet, reserved, and clearly besotted by his wife.

>>.p.187

. . .

Nicole Dunne is naked. Her eyes are closed. The air in the room is cold but her body feels warm. Sweat trickles behind her neck. She sweeps her leg out in an arc along the hard futon and feels soft skin, a bony foot. She caresses it with her toes. A tuft of wiry hair at the crest of the bridge scratches the pad of her toe. Bruno is smoking one of her cigarettes.

"Since when do you smoke?" she says. Her voice is smooth and husky.

"I smoke in the winter."

"Jesus," she says. "We've known each other through a change of seasons."

"Two," he says. "We met in June."

"It's December, that's—" she counts out the months on one hand. Bruno draws on the long white cigarette. "These are gross," he says. "How can you smoke these?" The sweat has begun to cool down her back. She shivers.

"I suppose I have to get into that goddamn shower," she says, standing. "I should install a real shower in here for you. If I had any actual money I would." Bruno smiles.

"That's a good one," he says, noticing the fat on her arms and thinking of the smooth limbs of the girls he usually has. What the hell is he doing? It isn't just the joke of this Chanel-clad socialite straddling him in his freezing studio, though that's part of it. It's a combination of reasons twisted up in his head like a ball of tape. He suddenly feels terribly lonely.

Nicole feels the shock of frigid water on her belly and rapidly scrubs between her legs and under her arms with a cracked sliver of soap. She lets the water run down her back for a second, shrieking, then steps out onto the filthy mat, grabbing a damp towel from a nail in the wall. Weak light glows through a dusty slit of a window, illuminating stacks of paintings separated neatly by wooden slats. Nicole owns three of Bruno Sikes's paintings. They have doubled in value since she bought them.

They met at a fund-raiser for a small downtown museum. Nicole was nervous and felt out of place in this hip crowd. She was speaking loudly, drinking too much wine, worried she was going to say something boring. Bruno walked right up to her, his long black hair shining around his shoulders, his dark eyes on her breasts. She guessed at his age—twenty-eight, twenty-nine.

"I'm Bruno Sikes," he said.

"I know," she said. "That woman over there just told me you're about to be famous."

"She's a moron."

Nicole laughed. She could see her husband at the other end of the room talking to another man. His arms were folded over his chest, his legs spread. He was frowning.

"I'd like to see your paintings," Nicole said to Bruno. "They're so controversial."

Nicole had a way of making everything she said sound a little bit dirty.

"They all look like you fifteen years ago," he said.

"Is that supposed to be an insult?"

"You'll see."

A week later she went to his studio for a visit. She chose three paintings of blond women with big blue eyes and plump breasts, called his dealer to reserve them. When she hung up the phone he had his hand on her waist.

. . .

She walks down the unfinished hallway wrapped in the towel, her arm brushing against exposed two-by-fours. Several color Xeroxes fanned out on a table catch her eye. There is an image of a fragile girl Nancy's age, white-blond hair, dark eyes, delicate limbs, standing beneath a tree.

"Who is this?" Nicole asks, holding up the image and waving it at Bruno through the door.

"An ex-girlfriend of mine."

Nicole squints at the image. "What was she called?"

"Louisa."

"I hope she was a little older when—"

"Could you put that back on the table?" he says, sitting up, cutting her off. Nicole replaces the Xerox, walks back into the bedroom, and dresses, turning her back, struggling into the snug pink skirt, the jacket. She feels his cold gaze on her and faces him, screwing in an earring.

"I don't know when I'll be able to come down again," she says.

Fine rain is falling as she stands peering west on East Houston Street, her arm up, gold charm bracelet slid over a silk sleeve, no cab in sight. A large man with a bushy beard strides purposefully by her and halts abruptly in front of a fire hydrant. Nicole turns to look at him, her arm still up. The man is glaring at the hydrant, hand on his hip. Anxiety grabs at her. Her chest constricts.

"Get me out of this fucking neighborhood."

A truck speeds by. She imagines one of the truck's' tires unpeeling from its wheelbase, rolling crazily down the middle of the street. A white car swerves to get out of the way, crashes onto the sidewalk like a wave. She sees it as a flash of light, feels the jolt as it hits her.

She lies in the street bleeding, ripped open. The man at the hydrant runs up to her, kneels by her, takes her hand in his filthy fingers. She looks into his mad face. He had a life once too.

A free taxi crossing the Bowery moves slowly toward her, its top light glowing in the rain. She stretches out her hand to the light.

Please, she thinks. *Please God.*

. . .

Nicole is looking out the window as the cab makes its jerky ascent up Madison Avenue. At Sixtieth Street, she takes her wallet out of her purse. It falls open on her lap. A photograph of Nancy shines beneath a sheath of plastic. She is smiling slightly, her eerie blue eyes staring up at her mother through the gloom of the taxicab. Nicole strokes the plastic cover with her fingertips as a familiar, forbidden thought rises in her brain: Nancy isn't lovable. She is calculating, capricious, untruthful, cold. Nicole takes a crisp twenty from the wallet and snaps it shut. Christ. How could she think it. What kind of mother. She leans back and remembers the smell of Nancy's little neck when she was a baby and the nurse would bring her downstairs after her bath. She smelled of powder and cinnamon.

The cab passes the Lowell Hotel. Nicole imagines telling the cab to stop, getting out, taking a room. Sending for her things. Excising herself from their lives like a tumor. A forty-three-year-old blond with spongy thighs living in a hotel. That's attractive. And he'd fight her for every penny. She could lose Nancy, the house in the Hamptons, maybe the apartment. She's seen it before. Wives aren't guaranteed a thing anymore. All there is to do is wait.

. . .

Steven Dunne is staring into the bathroom mirror. He is beginning to look like a wax replica of himself. He remembers a day long ago when the beauty of his own face held him spellbound for half an hour. The first time he saw his wife's face she was laughing. Now he remains motionless in order to keep from killing her. With a little energy he could kill everyone he has ever met.

Behind him on the wall there is a black-and-white photograph of a boy breaking a horse. The animal is rearing up, its back legs tied. The boy is pulling on the rope with strong slender arms. His eyes are screwed up against the light. Steven Dunne remembers the exhilaration of that day. His hands were rubbed raw by afternoon.

He takes his thumb and presses it into his chest, over his heart. He wants there to be a lot of blood when it happens. He wants her to have to deal with it.

. . .

Nancy is handing garments to Sarah Green as she undresses for her bath. Nicole knocks once and steps into the bathroom, her blond hair gleaming.

Mommy has her party face on.

Nancy hears the rustle of taffeta as her mother comes close and kisses her on the head.

"You can watch one hour of television but then you have to read two chapters of your book. Sarah can read one of them to you. Then lights out by nine o'clock, no dancing till dawn tonight, baby child." Sarah Green chuckles. Nicole shoots her an accomplice's wink.

"Can I have an ice cream after my bath?" Nancy asks.

"You already had flan, didn't you?"

"I know, but it was a little one."

"All right. Be good, Sweetie," says Nicole.

"Good night, Mommy," says Nancy.

Her father puts his head in the door. He is wearing a tuxedo.

There is something wrong with his face.

Nancy is suddenly frightened. She runs up to her father and clings to his silk jacket, whimpering, "Don't go, don't go . . ." Her father looks down at her arms around his waist, her naked back. He grabs her wrists; her skin feels strange against his palms, as if he were gripping his own numb limbs. He wills himself to pay attention, pries her hands from the cloth gently, mumbling, "Come on now." Sarah Green is watching. Her eyes meet Nicole's. Nicole looks back at Nancy, feeling guilt and irritation.

"Nancy," Nicole says. "We have to go." Nancy feels the hot tears on her face, soft cloth on her cheek. Her heart is falling.

"No," she says. She clutches her father's jacket; the women tighten the circle around her. They will catch hold of her arms, her legs. Lay her down on the bed screaming. Her parents will leave anyway. She's tried it before. They always leave. Her arms drop to her sides.

"Good girl," her father says, stepping back and looking down at his jacket. Two water spots on the silk are already shrinking. Soon they will be gone.

. . .

The lifeguard's name was Greg. Ever since the day he tried to save her, Nancy had been aware of his presence looming above her as she swam. Occasionally when she looked up at him he was watching her. One morning the air was dense with fog and Nancy was the only kid who'd shown up for swimming class. As she came out of the changing room she automatically looked up at the lifeguard's chair. Greg was at his station, nearly obscured by mist. Nancy sat down at the edge of the pool and dangled her feet in the water, straightening out her legs slowly and watching the thick sheets of water ripple down her skin, making it look as if she were encased in ice.

I hear a creaking in the sky. I don't have to look up, I know he is coming down. He sits down next to me.

You're a good swimmer, Nancy, how old are you?

Eight.

My cheeks feel hot. He stands. I don't look up.

It was weeks later, near the end of summer, that Nancy saw the lifeguard alone again. She was walking backward along the beach outside her house, watching her parents having a picnic with two other couples. A photographer from *House and Garden* magazine was there. His name was Chico. Nancy had been allowed to stay at the picnic for fifteen minutes. Now she was to go play with the nanny at the house. Nancy kept walking backward, her eyes on her parents. She passed the entrance to the house. They didn't notice. She kept walking until her parents were very small, then turned and ran.

I come to a cove hidden from the rest of the beach by three walls of grassy dune. I will play here. I round the corner. He is here. He is sleeping. He is lying on his stomach like a seal. I walk over to him and sit next to him. Droplets of water glisten on his brown skin like diamonds. I take a fistful of sand and hold it over his back, loosening my fingers. A fine mist of sand fans out in the breeze and dusts his shoulder.

He opens his eyes.

Nancy?

Hi.

What are you doing?

Nothing. I was going to play, and then I saw you.

He sits up and looks out toward the sea. The sky is blue but there is a big cloud the shape of a couch in the distance. A spray of water falls from it like a veil.

You have to be careful swimming in the sea.

I know.

Where are your parents?

He lies down again and props up his head with a fist.

Down the beach. They're eating oysters.

I make a face. He is staring at me. His face looks heavy. I make a well in the sand, and I notice something moving in his bathing suit. I know what is in there but I didn't know it could move.

Do you want to touch it?

Okay.

I reach out to the purple-flowered swim trunks. I push the thing in and it bounces back like rubber. I draw my hand back.

Like this.

He takes my hand and guides it up and down. He takes his hand away and I keep doing it because I want to see what it's doing to his face: his skin is swelling and going red and his jaw drops like he's surprised.

Suddenly he turns onto his side, away from me. I hear my father calling me. I run down to the sea. The ocean has gone dark; a wind rises up, whipping my hair back from my face. My father is down the beach, calling my name. I run to him.

Where were you?

Making a sea wall.

You were supposed to go straight to the house.

Fat drops splash down on the water. The rain feels like needles on my skin. I look up at my father. For a second I think he made it rain on me.

Come on!

He takes my hand. We run to the house. My mother and the rest of them are running ahead, lugging the picnic things and laughing. Chico is taking pictures.

. . .

Later, Nancy sat curled up in an armchair sipping hot chocolate, a towel around her hair, and watched the storm through the plateglass window. The thought of what happened with the lifeguard made her squirm. She tried to push it away but it kept coming back. So she decided to pretend that what happened in the cove was a made-up story. She kept

thinking of it that way until one day, months later, she remembered it in gym class and wasn't sure it had happened
at all.

. . .

Once Nancy's parents have left for the evening, Sarah
Green starts asking Nancy questions.

"Anything interesting happen in school today?"

"I'm getting that skirt I want," says Nancy.

"Really?"

"It costs like three hundred dollars."

"That's a lot of money," says Sarah.

"My mother told me yesterday we have to think about
money," says Nancy, taking her little white mouse Henrietta
out of her cage.

"Why do you have to think about money?" asks Sarah, leaning forward in her chair. Nancy pauses, petting the mouse.

"Because soon we'll be so poor that we'll be as poor as
you," she says. "We won't have anything, not even enough to
feed ourselves, and my mother is going to have to sell all her
clothes."

"Why do you think that?"

Nancy turns and puts the mouse back in its cage.

Sarah writes down everything Nancy does and says in a
little red notebook once the child is asleep, and then types it

into her computer when she gets home on Monday. Sarah thinks she may be on to an interesting case. Nancy has opened Sarah Green's little red notebook, and though she can't make out all the words she knows it is about her. She likes being watched by Sarah. She wishes Sarah would guess all her secrets.

"Why don't you draw a picture?" Sarah asks. Nancy slides into Sarah's lap and draws a headless, elegantly dressed female body walking a dachshund. Sarah asks to keep only her most gruesome drawings, so Nancy always tries to make really disgusting ones for her. Blood cascades down from the severed neck; there is a puddle of it on the ground. The dachshund is lapping it up. When she is done, Sarah asks urgently, "Can I have that one?"

"Sure," says Nancy, smiling proudly, leaning back into Sarah's bony chest. Sarah buries her nose in the child's thick hair and kisses her, surprising herself.

. . .

I wake up in the middle of the night and listen, trying to separate the sounds. I can hear the heat hissing out of the radiators, the hum of the refrigerator in the kitchen, the muffled honking of horns through the shut window. But there is another sound. I get out of bed and stand up. I turn the doorknob, holding my breath. My door is always supposed to be shut. *I pull the door away from the frame very slowly. It makes a swooshing sound as it skims the carpet. The hallway is dark, but at the end of it I can see that the living room is glowing. The curtains are open. I hear the sound again. Somebody is crying. I am scared. I walk down the hall. The living room is empty. I look around the corner. My father is kneeling on the floor by the fireplace, hunched over, his head bowed, as if he were trying to squeeze himself into a tiny doorway. He is crying. I hear ice clink in a glass. I step back. My mother comes into the room. She is in her black silk evening dress.*

My father keeps sobbing in a little ball. My mother puts down a drink on the coffee table beside him and sits on the couch.

Steve.

My mother sighs and looks away. It feels like she is looking right at me but she doesn't see me. My mother laughs, not a real laugh.

If they could see us now.

My father crawls toward my mother. My mother puts her hand on his head. He pulls himself up onto the couch. Then he falls down on her. It is too dark to see. They look like one thing struggling, like an animal trying to get out of a trap and moaning.

Nancy turns and walks back down the hall to her room, shutting the door very softly and switching on the light. The walls are painted lavender. The barn doors of her plastic farmhouse are open and a flood of dolls, some naked, some with one arm, their blond hair frayed, legs splayed, tumble from the narrow doorway like they were being vomited up. Nancy sits on the bed and looks at the photographs of horses on the walls, the blue and red ribbons she has won. The white mouse noses its way out of a pile of wood shavings, stands on its hind legs, and drinks from the metal dropper, working its jaw, its tiny pink hands gripping the mesh of the cage. Nancy stares at the mouse, a high-pitched sound in her ear.

She leans over and opens the cage, edges her hand in through the narrow door. The mouse climbs up her fingers, begins to crawl along her narrow wrist. Nancy draws her hand out of the cage and sets the creature down on her pillow, gently twisting her arm out from under its body. She observes as the mouse sniffs the pillowcase with abrupt, nervous movements, then pauses for a moment, its nose in the air.

With a sudden jerking movement Nancy folds the pillow in two, like a book with a live marker. Her arms feel stiff as wood, her palms drawn together like magnets. Her mind is motionless, stuck, the high note fraying, expanding in her ear. She feels the mouse's panicked wriggling faintly through layers of down.

Gradually the struggling slows, stops.

Nancy opens the pillow very slowly. The mouse is twitch-
ing, its eyes open. Panicked, Nancy takes it by the tail and
tosses it into the cage, withdrawing her hand swiftly and locking the door.

The little white body is still. So still. What will she say.
Please.

The room around her seems to be going dark. Her hand
on the cage looks foreign to her. Tears trickle down the side
of her nose, along her lower lip, into her mouth. She wishes
the dark would swallow her, leave no trace.

. . .

Something scrapes the floor of the cage. Nancy pitches
forward, presses her face against the wire mesh. The tiny
white head rises, sinks, then rises again. The mouse sits up
weakly, its nose bobbing in the air.

Nancy leaps up, runs through the bathroom to Sarah
Green's door. Very softly she tries the knob; it is unlocked.
She opens the door. Sarah is facing the wall, curled on her
side. Her red notebook is beside the bed, her clothes in a
messy pile on the chair. Nancy runs over to the bed. The
window is open. A gust of air blows into the room. Nancy
shivers. Carefully she lifts the comforter, feeling the warm
air rising from Sarah's body. She slips under the covers and

puts her arm around Sarah's waist, pressing her face into her back. Sarah mutters something and pats Nancy's hand. Nancy closes her eyes. She feels so heavy.

I am in a little boat on the tip of a red wave. The wave is growing. I feel dizzy. I am moving toward the sky.

Paula

Rain hammered the windshield. The wipers whipped back and forth, their beat like a frantic heart. She had pulled off the road to get a donut and coffee half an hour before. Now she sat staring.

The kid shifted in his seat. Paula turned to look at him, surprised by his presence for a second. Fourteen or fifteen, a runt, a runaway maybe. She had picked him up out of the pouring rain. He had a red welt on the side of his face.

"You're my first hitchhiker."

"You never picked anyone up before?"

"No."

"Why'd you pick me?"

He had been standing by the side of the highway outside Poughkeepsie, his back rounded like a freezing dog, brow furrowed, filthy pants flapping around skinny legs, thin jacket a couple of sizes too small. His thumb wasn't even out. She would have driven by him. But she had known he was a sign.

"I'm gonna get more donuts," she said. "Stay in the car, okay?" She felt around in her satchel for her wallet, pawing through several leaves of rough drawing paper, loose cigarettes, two frayed paperbacks, a bra. The bottom of the bag was covered in crumbs. At last she grasped her wallet, opened the car door, and ran up the concrete steps. Then she paused, remembering the keys in the ignition. She turned to look at the kid. He was hunched in his seat, staring out at the rain. She imagined him starting the dented old car, driving off, leaving her stranded.

The air in the donut shop was warm, thick, sweet. A woman with a child on her hip was being handed a fragrant, waxy bag. She opened her fist into the palm of the girl at the register, released a pile of coins. Exact change. The child on her hip stared at Paula, eyes glassy with sleep, as she was carried out the door. The blond girl at the register looked up, saw a very young woman with short, peroxide-white hair, big dark eyes, smudged mascara.

"A box of honey-glazed and two large coffees please," Paula said.

"Weren't you just here?" The girl was smiling.

"I'm pregnant," said Paula. Deadpan. The girl wasn't sure if she was serious, started to laugh, then stopped. Turned to get the donuts. Paula remembered the kid, looked out the window. He was still there.

In the car she opened the rain-spattered cardboard box. The kid reached out his left hand gingerly and took a donut. Then he turned away from her and chewed.

"Where do you want to be dropped off?"

"Where are you headed?"

"Upstate."

"Upstate's fine."

The rain was crashing down on the windshield now. It was like being in a car wash. She drove at a creeping pace, leaning forward over the steering wheel, squinting through the thin membrane of glass that separated her from the deluge. She imagined the windshield breaking, water pounding down on her, filling her nose, her throat. She pulled in a deep breath, glanced at her watch. Seven o'clock. Vincent had probably called the police.

They drove for an hour without saying a word. She stopped for gas, glanced at the kid. He was looking out the window, gnawing at the skin on the forefinger of his left hand, around the cuticle. He felt her gaze and put his hand flat on his lap. The skin around his nails had been gnawed raw. She watched as two tiny beads of blood rose to the surface of his skin. If a third one came up, she thought, she would go see her mother.

She turned off at the exit, drove the half hour to the house, deep into the landscape. She felt the kid's eyes on her.

"I'm making a stop. You can stay in the car or you can come in. Later I'll take you back to the highway." The sky was clearing.

A dirt driveway led them through dense woods to the house.

"You want to come in?"

"I guess not," said the kid. He hadn't moved. He was slumped in his seat.

In the kitchen the television was on mute. The news. Paula looked around at the heavy skillets hanging on the walls. Her eyes were drawn to an empty space where a picture of her father had been. She could still see it: he was standing in front of the house holding two fishing rods. Paula had been fishing with her father for the first time that day. He had stared into the water for a very long time without saying a word. Paula gripped her pole with both hands and watched the tall reeds at the edge of the lake swaying in the wind, each fluffy tip moving at its own pace, like spectators craning their necks, trying to get a better view of an accident. There was a sharp tug on her line.

"Daddy—" Her father took the pole from her, winding the reel back swiftly. Paula stared at the flat black water, her heart pounding. The fish broke the surface like a rocket, dangled over their heads flailing. Her father reached up to stop its swinging, yanked the hook out of its mouth and tossed it onto the floor of the boat.

"Dinner for one," he said. The fish curled itself up, its gills distended, and started slapping its head on the rough wood.

"Oh it's horrible. Throw him back. Throw him back Daddy please! Please!"

Her father grabbed the writhing fish and held it up in his big hand, grinning. Paula watched its pink, mute mouth opening and closing, tears streaming down her cheeks. Suddenly her father's face went slack. His skin darkened. His arm jerked up. She flinched, then saw the fish arc through the air, sparkling silver in the light. It hit the water with a little splash. Paula leaned over the boat staring as its dark form undulated and dissolved into the lake. She looked up at her father. His eyes were shining. A week later he left for New Mexico with her mother's best friend.

"Mom? Mom!" She heard rushed footsteps on the stairs. Her mother came in wearing a gray vest over her pajamas, her hair in a long braid down her back.

"Oh my God, it is you, I thought I was hallucinating!" She took Paula in her arms and squeezed her hard. "What an amazing surprise! Are you all right?" Paula's leather jacket was covered in a fine spray of mud. The knees of her jeans were dirty, torn.

"I'm fine."

"You want some coffee? Peter will be down in a minute."
That was a warning.

"Isn't he usually at work by now?"

"If you call first it's easier."

"I'm just stopping by. Is that all right?"

"Of course it is." Paula's mother's boyfriend stalked in.
He was bald, with a ponytail.

"Paula. You changed your hair again."

"Yup."

"What brings you up our way?"

"I came to see my Mom."

"How much do you need?" He poured himself some
coffee, legs planted far apart. He looked confident, propri-
etary. Paula stared at the table.

"I'm gonna go get geared up," Peter said. He kissed her
mother and left the room whistling.

"What is it, honey?" her mother asked, sitting down beside her.

Paula pulled the sleeve of her sweater up and examined
her arm. A bruise was starting to form, from her wrist to her
elbow. Her mother drew in her breath.

"What happened?"

"I was in an accident."

"In the car?"

"I was walking next to this guy, and he got run over."

"Oh my God."

"We had just traded places. Sixty seconds earlier and it would have been me."

"Start at the beginning, Paula."

Paula looked out the window. A tree was waving silently in the wind, its leaves shimmering crazily. It looked like it was warning her of something.

"Vincent and I had a fight."

It was a fight about laundry. She had started it. He hadn't let the clothes stay in the dryer long enough at the Laundromat. The damp underwear draped over the radiators filled her with panic. She hadn't told him about the baby. She knew it would get real if she said it. She didn't want it to get real. She was twenty-one.

They had met two years earlier. She was slumped on a bench in Tompkins Square Park, her head resting on the grimy bag beside her. Her eyes were closed, her hands cradled in her lap like an open basket. She felt something cool and hard in her palm. She opened her eyes, sat up. It was a perfect green pear. She looked up and a black-eyed man was standing there. Skin the color of chestnuts.

"You looked like you were waiting for something."

She put the pear to her mouth and bit into the tender, grainy flesh, then stood up and walked beside him. They slept

in his bed all afternoon, holding each other constantly, turning over in the sheets like synchronized swimmers. She felt
he had been drawn across the sky, all the way from Haiti, to
find her. A year passed. Gradually, imperceptibly, an invis-
ible sheath was closing over her mind. She began to sleep at
the edge of the bed, her leg dangling over the side. It was as
if she missed her loneliness. The night of the fight she left
the apartment at ten and drove into Manhattan, called her
friend Fiona from the corner of Spring and Broadway.

"I went to a club with Fiona and Jackie," she said to her
mother. "We got there and I started talking to this guy. Don't
disapprove, okay, or I'm not telling you."

"I didn't say anything."

When she got to the club the music was so loud she felt
the bass line in her collarbone. She started dancing with
Fiona, noticed a tall man with shaggy blond hair standing
under a red light. Everyone around him was shrouded in blue.
When she got to the bar he stepped back to make space for
her, into the blue. She looked down at her hand glowing red.
The tall man offered her a drink, yelling over the music. She
shook her head, bought her own. The whiskey hit her in the
gut; she hadn't eaten. She asked the bartender for peanuts.
The tall man offered her a bowl out of her reach. He had an
accent. She looked up at him.

"Where are you from?" she asked.

"Norway." He was wearing a dark suit. He looked like an elegantly dressed Viking. His cheekbones were so broad he was almost ugly. His skin was pockmarked. He had enormous hands. They talked. He said he directed music videos in L.A., told her which ones. She'd liked them.

"What do you do?" he asked.

"I'm a waitress. I sort of write, I used to paint," she said. "I think I'm going to be one of those people with a lot of potential who never really takes off."

He laughed. "Those are always the best people." His eyes were very clear, very blue.

They talked about music, porn, earwax, marriage, and furniture. There was a recognition between them, and tension. She kept thinking maybe he was the reason why she'd come here.

"He said he'd walk me to my car, which was down on Canal," she said to her mother.

As they walked, they continued to talk and laugh, but a feeling of melancholy settled in Paula. She shouldn't have done this to Vincent. She wanted to go home and start trying to forget about this guy.

"We were just talking, and a car went by fast—muddy water splashed all over me. And he said the man should walk on the outside, you know, so the woman doesn't get muddy. It was like a joke."

He touched her wrist and drew her toward him. They changed places.

"So we switched places. Then I heard a noise, like a shot, and I said was that a shot? And he said no, and we kept talking. And then I felt a smack on my arm. And the guy *vaporized*. There was a crash. I was on my face on the street and I sat up and looked around. There was a shoe in the middle of the street. A car was smashed into the building down the block. And then I saw the guy like draped over this parking meter."

"Oh, Paula." Her mother had her hand over her mouth.

"It was supposed to be me, Mom. Or it wasn't I guess, that's what I can't figure out." She laughed. Her mother just looked at her. "The place was crawling with cops and ambulance guys trying to pry the guy off his parking meter, and this one policeman kept asking me if the bartender that served us was male or female. I was having trouble breathing. At one point the cop talking to me turned away and I just ran. I ran all the way to my car and started driving. I don't know what I'm doing here. I just know I'm not meant to go home."

"What do you mean, you're not meant to go home?"

"I want to get an underwater camera," said Paula earnestly. "I'm going to get one." There was a pause. The phone rang. Paula's mother waited a moment, got up, and went into the next room.

"Vincent!" She liked him. "She's here." She walked into
the kitchen carrying the portable phone.

"It's Vincent," she said.

Paula took the phone.

"Hi."

"Paula, I called the police! I've been going out of my
mind!"

"I was going to call you," she said.

"Great. Thanks. Fiona said you stayed on to talk to a guy
at some club."

"Yes," she said.

"What happened?"

"Nothing," she said.

"When are you coming back?"

"I don't know." Her voice sounded disembodied to her,
foreign. Her mother had retreated from the room to give her
privacy, but now Paula saw her hovering outside the door.

"I don't believe this."

"Okay," she said into the receiver.

"Okay what?"

"Me too," she said. "See you later." She hung up. Peter
walked in and peered out the window, hitching up his tool
belt.

"Who's that kid in your car?"

"He needed a ride."

"You picked up a strange kid?" Peter had his hands on his hips.

"Yes," she said, looking him in the eyes.

"Maybe he's cold," said her mother.

"I left the engine running," said Paula. Peter let a great rush of air out of his throat.

"She left the keys in the car with some runaway?!" he said, turning to her mother, an eyebrow arched.

"It isn't safe, honey," said her mother softly. Peter pulled on his jacket.

"I'm going to work," he said, taking the cordless phone and smacking it onto its cradle in the next room, then sticking his head through the doorway. "Paula. You probably won't be here when I get back, so I'll say good-bye now." Paula sat staring at the table. When he'd gone she looked up at her mother.

"He's exactly like Dad, only uglier."

"You just make him defensive."

Paula laughed briefly. Her heart was racing. Her mind was being flooded with images, ideas. She wanted to write. To paint. She felt electric. Her knee was jiggling up and down. She picked a steak knife from a jug on the table and let the point dangle over her hand.

She could feel the thing inside her, an ache without pain. She imagined it sucking the seconds out of her life as it built itself up cell by cell, ineluctable, devouring. Mouth. Lungs.

Spine. Connected to her by a thread of membrane, like the kind you find in fertilized eggs. She saw an image of herself pushing a stroller. She was pushing it up and down the street. That's all she did all day. Mothers seemed like slaves to her. Happy, tired slaves.

"I'm pregnant but I'm not having it."

She let the steak knife drop. The point hit her at the fleshy base of her thumb and bounced off. Her mother drew in her breath. Paula touched the little indentation on her skin and held up her hand to her mother.

"See?" she said. "Nothing."

"What do you mean *see*?"

"I don't know, I haven't figured it out yet."

"How pregnant?"

"I really have to start writing some of these ideas down," Paula said. The phone rang. Paula's mother went to the next room to answer it. Paula got up and walked out the door.

When she got into the car the kid was shivering.

"You should have turned the heat up," she said, backing out the driveway.

Her mother ran out of the house, shaking the phone over her head. Paula waved at her, turned the car around, and stepped on the gas.

They sped along the winding roads, back to the highway. She stopped by the side of the road, felt a wave of energy hit

her from inside—a thrill of fear, like when a roller coaster
has tipped down and starts gathering speed. She told herself
if the next car that drove by on the highway was yellow, red,
or blue, the kid was supposed to stay in the car. If it was any
other color, he needed to go back on the road. She let the
car idle at the edge of the highway for a few minutes. No traffic. Finally a white truck appeared over the horizon.

"Okay," she said. "Time for you to go."

There was sweat on his forehead. His eyes were clear and
green, the pupils very small and black. She looked into her
wallet. She had been to the bank machine the night before
and taken out a hundred dollars. She had eighty left. She
unpeeled a twenty, then another ten, and handed them to
him.

"Here," she said. "Good luck."

"Thanks," said the kid, taking the bills in his grimy,
bitten-up fingers.

"Do you have anyplace to go?" she said.

"My uncle . . ." he said. He was speaking very softly.

"You've been a good travel companion," she said, offer-
ing her hand. He reached out to her with his right hand and
the sleeve of his small jacket was pulled three quarters of the
way up his forearm. The arm was horribly bruised. He tried
to yank his hand away, but she held on to it and pushed the
sleeve farther back. There were lacerations on the inside of

his arm. Little bits of flesh had been ripped away. It looked like someone had used a fishhook. He pulled the hand free.

"What else?" she said. "What else did they do?"

He stared into his lap.

"Open your jacket," she said. "Open it up, I want to see something." He didn't move. She reached for the zipper and he pushed her away. She pulled the cloth down around his neck, saw the edge of a wound, bruises.

"I'm taking you to the hospital," she said.

He opened the car door and nearly fell to the ground. She grabbed at his jacket; he jerked himself free and ran out along the highway. She got out and went after him. He could barely run. She grabbed him, put her arms around him. He cried out in pain.

"Okay," she said. "No hospital. No hospital, Okay? I'll just take you to a pharmacy. We'll get some disinfectant for those cuts and you'll be on your way. Just calm down." He walked back to the car beside her, her hand gripping the cloth of his jacket.

The drugstore in Catskill had a front on it that hadn't changed since the fifties. A little bell tinkled as she walked in with the kid beside her. The middle-aged pharmacist emerged from the back room, her face dusted with yellowish powder.

"Paula Friedrich!" she said.

"Hi, Mrs. Toron," said Paula. She'd come to this pharmacy all her life, till her mother got the new boyfriend.

"You're in Manhattan now, aren't you?"

"Brooklyn."

"That's right. I assumed you were off at college all this time, but then your mother said you were in the city. Wesley is a senior at Syracuse."

The kid shifted from one foot to the other. Mrs. Toron turned to him. He looked filthy, homeless. She wasn't smiling anymore.

"I'm kind of in a hurry, Mrs. Toron."

"What can I do for you?"

"I need gauze bandages, tape, hydrogen peroxide, and arnica gel if you have it. And cotton balls." Her voice was trembling. Mrs. Toron gazed at her curiously. Paula felt her eyes fill with tears. She walked away quickly and stared at the toothbrushes. Mrs. Toron went to gather the items.

. . .

The motel room was dim, with textured walls and a painting of a harbor above the bed. The kid looked around warily, his back against the open door.

"I just want to get you cleaned up," she said. "Sit down."

The kid sat down stiffly on the bed, his hands resting beside him, his eyes on the shiny glass of the television screen.

She locked the door, unzipped his jacket, and pried it off him gently. He wasn't wearing a shirt. His chest and back were covered in blackish-purple bruises tinged with green. They looked like thunderclouds gathering under his skin, ready to rain blood. Long, thin wounds glistened on his shoulders, his back. He had been whipped.

"Oh my God," she said. "Oh Jesus." The kid stared at the television, his small mouth slightly open, his cheeks flushed red.

"Take off your pants," she said. The kid pulled down his pants and sat there in his underwear, staring at his legs. His ankles and calves had been lacerated, crosshatched with tiny wounds.

In a flash Paula saw the man from the club, that beautiful man, impaled on a parking meter like a broken doll. And she had left him there.

She led the kid into the bathroom and bathed his wounds with water, poured hydrogen peroxide on them and watched it fizz. She spread disinfectant onto the broken skin and arnica gel on the bruises. She taped white bandages to his skin. He let her touch him, watching her, wincing when she touched the wounds. She felt his eyes on her. Her cheeks went hot. Whenever she looked up he looked away. When she was done he walked into the bedroom, turned on the TV, lay down on the bed. Within seconds he was asleep.

She drew a blanket over him. He curled up under the covers, slid his thumb between his lips. Paula clamped her hand over her mouth and cried out silently. Hot tears trickled through her fingers. She picked up the phone and punched out her own number. He answered after one ring.

"Where are you?"

"In a motel."

"What the hell is happening? Are you fucking that guy from the club?"

"Vincent, no, listen. There's this kid, this little—I don't know, fifteen or something, this boy I picked up on the highway and it turns out he was beaten."

"What do you mean beaten?"

"Somebody tortured him, Vincent, they—he's like pulp."

"So—you're in a motel with that kid?"

"I had to help him."

"I'm coming to get you."

"He has no place to go. They'll kill him if he goes back to where he was."

"The welfare people will take care of him if we call them. You did the right thing. Just tell me where you are."

"He'll run away if we call anyone, I know he will. I can't leave him, I can't. Could I bring him home? Couldn't he stay with us for a while?"

"Are you crazy? We've got no space. You don't know this kid."

"Please. Please, please, please. I can't leave him. I can't." She wiped her nose with her sleeve. Her face was covered with tears and snot.

"Paula. Jesus."

"Something happened, baby I'm so sorry, but I was walking with this guy and we changed places and he got hit."

"What are you talking about?"

"The guy I met at the club. He got hit by a car. It was supposed to be me. Sixty seconds earlier and it would have been me. We changed places." In her mind she saw heavy drops of rain falling onto parched red earth, turning it to mud. "There has to be some reason for it, don't you see? If he hadn't met me he wouldn't be dead. This makes sense. It's a sign." The line was quiet for a while. Paula saw the rain washing the mud away. Underneath was something white and clean, like bone.

"So—you get someone killed, you save someone, you're even."

"Kind of."

"You're always trying to figure everything out, aren't you, the whole fucking universe," he said, but his voice was kind and sad. "Bring the kid. Okay? Bring the kid. He can sleep on the couch. We'll take care of him. Just come home. Please come home. I don't want you driving like this. Take the train. Take a cab to the train. I'll pick up the car. Paula? Paula, do you hear me?"

"Thank you," she said. Then she hung up.

When the kid woke up, she paid the bill and they got back in the car.

They drove to Poughkeepsie and stopped at the donut shop again. It was three o'clock in the afternoon by now. Paula parked and turned to the kid. He had his head back and looked relaxed, almost handsome now.

"What's your name?" she said.

"Kevin."

"I talked to my boyfriend. He said it was fine for you to come stay with us in Brooklyn for a while, till you're better, and we can figure out what to do. I can't let you out on your own like this. We'll take the train. I'm too tired to drive anymore. What do you say?"

"I'm gonna live with you?" She thought he might be smiling a little, but she wasn't sure.

"Just for a while. With me and my boyfriend. Till we straighten stuff out." The kid wasn't looking at her. His eyes were roving along the dashboard. It occurred to Paula that he had never looked her in the eye.

"What do you want for lunch?" she asked. "I'm getting a grilled cheese sandwich."

"I guess I won't have lunch just now," said the kid.

"I'll get you one for later," she said.

She took her wallet out of her bag and went into the donut shop. The line was long. She felt beat. She was having trouble keeping her eyes open.

That's when she heard the squeal. She turned around. Her car was backing up. She ran outside to see him turn it around and peel out onto the street. A bald man, a customer, followed her out. The kid ran a red light and he was gone.

"You little shit," she heard herself say.

"Want me to call the police?" asked the bald man.

"No," said Paula. "I know him."

The bald man shook his head and went back into the shop. Paula stood on the concrete steps. She felt unmoored, tricked. She didn't know what she was supposed to do now. She didn't know how to read the signs. They were like braille. She hoped the kid would be all right. It was so dangerous out there. She was suddenly terrified.

She felt herself, her life, edged by a great shadow which seemed to extend forever, like the ocean at night. Violence, disaster—they waited in that dark. That's where the kid had come from. It's where the man at the club had gone. One day—any day—she too would slip past its borders. But for now she was alive, with a person inside her! She could feel herself growing, cell by cell. This was real. It was the only thing that was real. She had someone to protect.

She turned and pushed open the glass door, breathing in the dense air of the shop. Two customers were sitting in booths. The blond girl stood behind the register, her back against the wall, arms folded, staring off. Paula walked toward her. It seemed to take a very long time, as if the counter and the girl behind it kept retreating as Paula approached. Finally she reached the orange counter. As she rested her palms on its smooth surface she was charged with an acute, almost painful happiness.

"Excuse me," Paula said softly, urgently. The girl focused on her slowly, then leaned toward her, elbows on the counter.

"Yes?" she said.

Paula looked into the girl's large, blue, inquisitive eyes.

"Could you tell me how to get to the train station?"

Acknowledgments

I would like to thank my friend and teacher, Honor Moore, for her time and her generosity; my parents for their enthusiasm; my agent Sarah Chalfant for her faith; my friends Michael Rohatyn and Barbara Browning for reading the stories and talking to me about them; Barbara Browning for the use of her poem, "Lets just sit at home with the cause," incorporated into the story "Bryna" (p. 119); Vicki O'Connell for helping make it possible for me to write; my husband for all his kindness, support, and advice; and Ronan, for everything.